Mary Andrews Denison

The Cuban Heiress

Or, the prisoner of La Vintresse

Mary Andrews Denison

The Cuban Heiress
Or, the prisoner of La Vintresse

ISBN/EAN: 9783744796521

Printed in Europe, USA, Canada, Australia, Japan

Cover: Foto ©Andreas Hilbeck / pixelio.de

More available books at **www.hansebooks.com**

THE

CUBAN HEIRESS:

OR,

𝕿𝖍𝖊 𝕻𝖗𝖎𝖘𝖔𝖓𝖊𝖗 𝖔𝖋 𝕷𝖆 𝕍𝖎𝖓𝖙𝖗𝖊𝖘𝖘𝖊.

LONDON:

GEORGE ROUTLEDGE AND SONS,
THE BROADWAY, LUDGATE.

THE

PRISONER OF LA VINTRESSE;

OR,

THE FORTUNES OF A CUBAN HEIRESS.

CHAPTER I.

ESCAPE AND DISAPPOINTMENT.

THE moonlight streamed broadly down upon the "Paseo De Ysabel Segunda"—the grand avenue of the city of Havana. Its two carriage-drives—its two walls for foot-passengers, glittered like silver in the splendors of the night; and the tree-branches that lined its sides were white with the glory of the full-orbed moon. The soft air was loaded with the scents of flowers that came from near and distant gardens. The blue field of stars glittered above, and the soft harmony of a full band of music, playing perhaps before the Governor's house, their farewell march, came gently on the night-wind.

Two figures lightly but hurriedly crossed the lower end of the beautiful avenue.

"We did well with the guards, Minerva, now we have passed all danger, and I shall soon put you on board—good heavens!"

The lady looked up hastily at this exclamation.

"Do you not see, Minerva, in the hurry and excitement, I have quite forgotten my portmanteau, containing all my papers—my drafts. In fact, I could not go without it. How unfortunate!"

"What *will* you do, dear Herman?" It was the musical voice of a young girl

. "There is but one thing I can do: put you on board and come back for it, then hasten to the ship, I don't think the tide is up. The boat that carries you will return with me, and it will not take thirty minutes. I *must* feel that you are safe."

"O Herman! it seems as if I dare not stay alone, and I am so fearful there may be trouble about your returning;" she said, half tearfully.

"Don't be afraid, dearest—the captain of the Eagle is a thorough gentleman, and I am well known here by most of the public authorities. Come, yonder is the boat, they are punctual—don't tremble so, my love."

"I fear—I hardly know what;" was the low reply.

"It is but natural;" returned the manly voice, "but you will soon feel safer when I am your protector. Here they are."

A boat approached the landing, propelled by two swarthy seamen.

"If I could only remain here till you return;" she murmured again.

"That would never do, Minerva. I'll see you to the vessel's side, however. What time do you set sail, men?"

"At twelve, to a second;" said one of the men.

"All right—I have an hour, then." Herman had pulled out his gold repeater—now he hastily put it back, secured Minerva in a comfortable seat, protecting her with lover-like energy against the up-coming of the restless waters as the sailors pulled oars lustily.

They reached the side of the black bulk. The captain's cheerful voice was heard.

"You are in good time, Mr. Goreham."

"Yes, sir; but I must ask the favor to be pulled back and waited for just ten minutes. By an unfortunate oversight I've left all my valuables, and this young lady, my cousin, of whom I spoke to you, will remain in your safe keeping."

"Ay, ay," responded the captain, "but I must limit you. Thirty minutes is the very longest I can spare the men, as I wish to set sail at twelve. Think you can do it?"

"I shan't be so long as that, captain, thank you. Now, be patient, darling," he whispered to the young girl as he helped her up

Another moment and the sailors were off, Mr. Herman Goreham keeping them company, while Minerva was conducted to the handsome cabin, and shown her own pretty state-room, by the stewardess.

Here she dismissed the woman and sat down, listening intently that she might catch the faintest flash of the oars on their quick return. Strangely enough, a drowsiness crept over her, and, giving way to the sudden languor, she fell asleep. When she awoke, a midnight darkness was around her, and for a moment she knew not where she was. A sullen sound and uneasy motion convinced her all at once that the vessel was under way, and had been perhaps for hours. A blank horror seized her—could she be alone? The clattering of the doors, the trembling of the ship, convinced her that she must be at sea, and in a high wind. She tried the door of her state-room, standing up as best she could. A sudden lurch sent her out into the cabin where she caught at the long table and strove to steady herself, that she might look about her. There was no sign of life there. The lantern swung dismally, and the bolts and casings creaked and groaned. Overhead were sounds of tramping feet and shouting voices. Totally unacquainted with a ship as she was, she gazed from end to end of the long cabin in utter dismay. Of course Herman was on board. He had come at the appointed time, supposed her asleep and would not disturb her. Which of the state-rooms, whose gilding looked so ghastly in the dim light, could be his? And yet he might just have knocked at her door. Perhaps he did; she must have slept very soundly not to hear. A feeling of desolation came over her in spite of her hope, that sent the tears gushing to her eyes. If she could only see one human face—if the captain could come in, or the stewardess. But this horrible rolling—this deathly faintness that now crept over her, shrouding as it were, soul and body in its hideous mantle. At any rate, she must get back to her state-room, and there listen for the captain. It could not be very long till morning if the vessel started at twelve, and she had probably slept some hours. The damp sea-wind chilled her, and an undefinable fear weighed down her spirits. She returned to her state-room and sank uneasily on her narrow bed. Ill as she felt herself growing, she did not call for assistance, but waited patiently. It was evident that the calm wind of the previous night had freshened into a gale. The ship leaped and plunged, and the ominous clattering as of ten thousand dishes, became every moment louder, while the shouts above, grew more hoarse and continuous.

Sad was that weary watching till the dawn, and welcome the first gray streak that slanted across the little state-room. Minerva attempted in vain to rise. The fearful giddiness of sea-sickness was upon her—the ominous sinking and depression that makes the malady seem tenfold more terrible. The gale had somewhat abated its violence—but the ship yet plunged from one large wave-top to the other.

Perplexing herself with wearying thought, she yet looked for some token from Herman. He might be as ill in his state-room as she was in hers, but surely he could send a message by the stewardess, or if there were other passengers, of which she was doubtful, by them or the captain.

The savory smell of coffee saluted her senses. Breakfast was being prepared, then; some one might think of her. She was not mistaken. In a few moments the door of her state-room opened, and the pleasant face of the stewardess appeared, shining through the steam of the beverage she held in her hand.

Minerva greeted her with a smile.

It was good to see a human countenance, even that of a stranger.

"How are you, miss?" the girl asked simply.

Minerva shook her head; her look was expressive.

"Ah, you are not used to the sea," said the girl—"get all right in good time. Take some strong coffee, that will make you better. Very pretty;" she added, nodding her head approvingly, as Minerva shook the long curling hair that had fallen from its fastenings, and hung in glittering curls all over the pillow.

The young girl smiled languidly and tasted the coffee. It gave her strength, for she lifted herself in the narrow bed, and her eyes grew brighter.

"The gentleman who came with me," she said, turning to the stewardess, who, with an admirable sea-gait, was placing the little state-room in order—"is he ill, do you think, this morning? He said he was never sick at sea, but then wo have had a terrible storm, have we not?"

"Very bad," replied the girl, who, though she was Spanish by birth, spoke excellent English; "but who do you mean, by the gentleman? You came alone; I saw no gentleman."

"Yes, I came over the vessel's side alone," said Minerva, "but my cousin was in the boat. He had to go back to the shore after some luggage he had forgotten, but he returned directly. If I had my pencil, I would write a message to him, and the steward could take it. It is strange that I have not heard from him before now."

The stewardess stood regarding the young girl with a glance of perplexity.

"Are you sure he came aboard?" she asked after a moment of silence.

Minerva trembled at her look—her heart gave a great bound as she spoke.

"Sure, of course; he was to sail this voyage with me: his trunks are on board. Why do you ask such a question?" she cried almost wildly. "Were you by when the boat came back?"

"No, not exactly;" said the stewardess; "but I was up in the cabin till long after the ship sailed, and I did see no one; but don't you be so pale and frightened, miss; I can very soon find out for you—the captain can tell. He might possibly have staid out, you see, to watch the ship getting under way; sometimes our passengers do, in particular the first night. Do not be afraid—I will go see directly. What number is his state-room?"

"Seventeen;" said Minerva, faintly, sinking back on her pillow, for the bare thought of such a trouble sent all the blood to her heart and made her sick with apprehension.

Meanwhile, Bandola, the stewardess, made her way to the state-room designated by Minerva. It was locked—plainly the captain or the person who had secured it, was in possession of the key. She tried it, called through the key-hole, and managed to peak in under the blinds that made the upper half of the door. There was nobody there, that was very evident.

The captain came in, wet with salt-spray, pale and en-
grossed. He had been hard at work since the gale sprang up.
Bandola went towards him; she was a great favorite with
him.

"Well, Banda, we're about through," he said. "Did the
storm frighten you? We had a fine taste of a tropical hurricane—one of the worst I ever saw. What?" he queried
sharply, not hearing what reply the stewardess made.

"That young man, sir, who came with the young lady; is he
anywhere on board?"

"Young man—on board—why of course he is," replied the
captain. "You mean Goreham—in his state-room, likely."

"Oh! no, captain, I have looked."

"And what business have you to be looking after young
men?" he asked, jocosely.

"Why, she, the young lady, sir, feels very bad about it.
She wanted me to, and I saw him not in the cabin, at all, last
night."

"The dickens!" said the captain, with energy. "Caul-
kings," he continued, turning to the first mate, who had come
in to his breakfast, "is Goreham on board?"

"No, sir;" said the man.

"What! not on board? What do you mean, sir?"

"The men staid nearly fifteen minutes after their time
against orders, sir," replied the mate, "and came back withou'
him. You had turned in, and, you remember. given charge or
no account to be disturbed. I felt a little uneasy when they
came back and nobody with them, but expected every mo
ment to see him alongside in some other boat, as he might ver
easily have done. Afterwards, in the hurry and confusion o
getting off, it did not occur to my mind, sir."

"Well, well," muttered the captain, his brow clouding
"this is an unfortunate thing; a mighty unfortunate thing
Here we have this young lady on our hands, and the poo
thing will be in a pretty mess. She'll fret herself to deatt
and who can wonder? There's certainly a mystery about i
Did he mean to stay?" he asked abruptly, as if questionin
himself. "No—Goreham's the soul of honor—at least I hav
always found him so. Well, well, this is a pretty pickle, t
be sure. Bandola, go to the lady and do what you can t

comfort her. Say that he was probably detained for some trifling thing by some of those confounded custom-house peo ple. It's very unfortunate, I'm sure, but it can't be helped, so I'll take breakfast."

But the worthy captain's spirits were low, that was easily to be seen. He ate and drank in silence, scarcely speaking to his companion.

CHAPTER II

SAD NEWS.

BANDOLA went back to the state-room, with a slow step. Minerva had managed to rise, and had nearly completed her toilet. She looked very pale, and her large, dark eyes were supernaturally bright with excitement and expectation. She fully expected to see Herman, as the little door opened. A slight flash mantled her cheek—a smile broke over her face. It was changed to a sudden look of disappointment—and that again to an expression of vague terror, for there was that in the kind face of the stewardess that made her heart sink.

"What! has he not come!" she asked.

"Lady—" the girl stopped there—not knowing how to communicate the rest.

"It can not be that he is not on board!" cried Minerva, growing every moment paler.

"He will come in another ship;" said Bandola, catching at the *vinaigrette* that laid on the pillow; "don't faint, lady; I'm sure he will come; he will take a vessel this very day; it will sail maybe, quicker than this; you will meet him there perhaps in New York."

"No—no—you can never know what reasons I have for fear—what terrible reasons;" the poor young girl almost gasped.

"But you will see him; you will certainly see him;" said the stewardess, the tears coming to her eyes. "Don't take on so, or you will be sick, and that will spoil your beauty;" she added, in the hope that an appeal to her woman's impulse might be successful.

"Oh! I am unfortunate;" wailed the poor girl—"*they* know that I have gone; they will waylay him; they will kill him; I shall never, never see him again. Is there no way for me to get back?—no way?—no returning ship? Oh, in mercy ask the captain; tell him I will pay him any price—and yet —it would be madness to return. Oh! why was I born to be the sport of fortune?"

All this time the stewardess was looking on pityingly, but wondering.

"Dear young lady," she said again, in her soft, soothing voice "it can't be helped; don't weep so—you will be very ill."

"I think the captain is to blame; it was cruel, cruel in him not to send the men back; I will never forgive him, never!" she cried, the Spanish blood mantling her cheeks—her large eyes flashing anger. "Was it a conspiracy? Is your captain a gentleman? an honest man?"

"What! Captain Wyllies? I will hear no word against him," cried the stewardess, almost angrily; "you have no right to blame him. He was worn out, and had to sleep, everybody was busy—they thought *he* would come in another boat, and it was all unfortunate and unhappy, but not on purpose. No one thought of such a thing. I am sorry for you, but you must say nothing against Captain Wyllies, because he is a good man. He would not do wrong for the whole world."

At that moment, the captain himself appeared. He looked quite pale and troubled.

"My dear young lady," he said, "this is very unfortunate; I assure you, I would give a great deal, if I were back in the harbor of Havana, this minute."

His frank, honest face, and real concern of manner, banished any lurking suspicion that had troubled her mind before.

"O captain! I can hardly think how to do or act," she said, her hands working over each other uneasily, her lips quivering.

"I think, under the circumstances, you had better let things take their course," he replied. "There is no way for you to return, unless I chance to speak a vessel bound to Cuba, and that is extremely improbable. If I do, however, and you should desire it, I will place you on board. Very likely, Mr. Gorcham was detained by some of the custom-house officers, who had, or thought they had, some other formalities to go through with, and he will take the first vessel bound for

home, so it will only make the difference of a few days, perhaps even hours. I advise you to look upon the bright side,
and be as cheerful as you can about it, every thing will come
out right. There were several vessels ready to sail to-day,
and be assured, he will take one of them. His anxiety will
be almost equal to your own."

"Oh, but he knows where I am," said Minerva, piteously.

" And for that reason, his mind will be so much the easier."

"While I am deplorably in the dark, with reference to his
fate," she added, the tears falling.

"I'll trust Goreham," said the captain, cheerily; " he's a
wonderfully keen young fellow, and not one of the sort to get
into scrapes. Don't you worry, we shall have a splendid run,
always do, with a storm at the outset; and in a week, trust
me, you will meet in the good city of Manhattan."

" But—but—he has enemies," sobbed the young girl brokenly.

A dim suspicion of the truth, forced its way into the mind
of Captain Wyllies.

This girl, though attired in thorough American costume,
needed only the vail, the coquettish fan, the rich full silks and
mantle of the Cubans, to transform her into a Spanish woman.
Hers were the wonderful eyes of that race, the rich, black,
luxuriant hair, the clear, olive complexion, a shade lighter,
perhaps, than the general line. The cousinship was, after all,
a ruse, the two were flying perhaps from jealous rivals, this
was the mystery. If so, there was certainly good cause for
the girl's alarm. Those Spanish haters strike quick and deep,
and fly justice. His pity grew, as the sad consequences of
the whole affair flashed across him. Perhaps, the poor child
was married, if so, and if harm had befallen him, a sad prospect stretched before her. Helpless and delicate, she seemed
entirely unfitted for sorrow, or for labor. These thoughts, of
course were his own, and rapid as lightning. They did not
show on the surface, in troubled glances. On the contrary,
the captain consoled her so much the more, as his own hopes
fell. He assured her that he could look out for her comfort,
and interest himself in her future fortunes. Bandola, he would
relinquish to her. "She is a good girl," he said, "a *protege*
of mine, and I'm going to educate her. She is not ignorant,

now," he added, laying his hand lightly on her head, ' so she may be some company for you. Cheer uu, young lady, 1 prophesy a renewal of your happiness, on your return. I feel almost certain that young Goreham will meet you there."

Unconsciously, the happy, earnest manner of the captain, infused new hope into the sorrowful heart of Minerva, and, though she could not quite divest herself of her melancholy forebodings, yet she did not allow herself to give way to them.

CHAPTER III.

THE GENERAL AND HIS HOUSEHOLD.

GENERAL LEINDRES DE MONSERATE was one of the grandees of Cuba. A little man, shrewd, and sharp of feature,
with nothing noticeable about his face, save a pair of magnificent black eyes, that, when he was pleased, wore a soft beauty,
rare in the eyes of man, but when deepened by passion, their
very repose was fearful. The general prided himself upon be-
longing to the *ancien regime*, and the scrupulous nicety of
his white cravat and spotless dress-coat accorded well with
his polished manners. His dwelling, though one of the
handsomest and most spacious on the island, did not look
pretentious on the outside. It was within, that his ideas of
magnificence all centered. The sun and the stars, could he
have brought them down, could hardly have contented him
with their brilliancy. The softest and most glittering fabrics,
composed the hangings of his rooms, every thing was elabo-
rately gilt, and yet good taste was predominant.

His conservatories were miracles of beauty and profusion,
in which birds from every clime sported among rare, strange
flowers, and fountains leaped in silvered spray to the crystal
roof, keeping along the margin of the water, a continuous musical vibration, that made one hold the very breath to hear.
The trees along the margins of his avenues glittered with
golden fruit, and in front of the house bloomed the Tahiti al-
mond, the mango, and the cedar.

General De Monserate, was literally the reigning head of
his little household. Even his sister, Mancha, an angular, little, black-eyed woman, who would domineer over a kitten if
she could find nothing else, was a mere cipher in her brother's
presence. The rest of his family consisted of a niece, partly
of Spanish, partly of English blood, a girl of seventeen, and a
young man, whose guardian the general was, a fiery, passion-

ate, and extremely elegant personage, and possessing an immense fortune in sugar estates and slaves. The general, in his own right, was poor; but through the favors of a will in his possession, obtained money enough to gratify all his nefarious and extravagant tastes. An old housekeeper, with drooping eyebrows, served doggedly under Senora Mancha; a bright-eyed octoroon was the dressing-maid of Senora Minerva. Von Carlos had his valet, and four or five black attendants, and the old general was seldom without his full complement of servants. The house was generally very gay, as the young senorita had not been long from one of the best American schools, and played and sang charmingly, besides possessing a variety of other accomplishments.

Preparations were evidently going on for a great party at the general's homestead. The servants were continually bearing hampers to and fro from the kitchen (which was a separate building) to the main residence. A happy set they seemed, showing huge ivories as they cracked their jokes, although they sweated under the apparent weight. The general's beautiful volante was oftener brought round than usual, sometimes occupied by the old gentleman himself, sometimes by the dashing Cuban, Don Carlos. Handsome as was this latter personage, an evil look permeated his countenance. His eyes, black and lustrous, pierced like stiletto's, and had all their murderous keenness. A thick, black mustache covered his lips, save one dark crimson line; his forehead was low but massively shaped, and in bright black clusters, the curls grouped themselves about it. Every one has seen such men, men whose faces they at the same time admired and detested, and from whose attentions, if of pure mind and correct princi ples, they instinctively shrank. Once, as Don Carlos drove out of the courtyard, he turned and lifted his hat, at the same time smiling and bending. The young senora sat in the window, from which she had been throwing crumbs to a pan of Barbadian doves. She returned the bow but at the same moment turned back with a pained look. Her maid, who was intelligent enough to make somewhat of a companion, noticed the motion.

"I wonder what wedding Signor Carlos is going to attend?" she said smilingly.

"Wedding!" the young girl spoke with pained surprise.

"I heard them talking about it, the general and Don Carlos, when they knew nothing of my being near. It is to take place to-night, at twelve."

"To-night, at twelve," murmured the senora, looking blankly at the octoroon; "to-night, at twelve, did you say? and my uncle?"

"Both of them," replied the girl, with a strange glance, "are to take part."

"They will never be so uncourteous as to leave their guests!" exclaimed Minerva, her color heightening.

"No, they will not need do that," was the response.

"What do you mean, Althea!" asked the young girl, now thoroughly roused, and not a little frightened. "There is something you wish to tell me, but dare not. Don't leave me in suspense. My uncle and that man have been plotting, I am sure of it; and oh, Althea, you would not see me suffer, if by a word you could prevent it."

"No, indeed, my dear mistress," said the girl, "you shall be saved, if any word of mine can do it. To-night, Padre Rouez is to be here, and Heaven only knows how it could be done, but you would be married."

Trembling from head to foot, the girl sprang from her seat, and began pacing the room.

"It would be monstrous," she muttered, "but they would not scruple; as Althea, says, it would be done,—I believe it. Now there is only one way to act, I must appear to acquiesce, or my doom is sealed. Little they think that by twelve o'clock, I shall be passing away from their hated influence. Althea, bring me pen and ink."

The girl placed both before her. Steadying her hand, and controlling the indignant impulse that almost shook her, so wronged did she feel herself, she wrote, as follows:

"HONORED UNCLE:

"I have overheard that I am to be married to-night, at twelve. This anticipation of an event, which for some time I have known you to consider quite near, should not be approached without due reflection. I ask, therefore, that you will allow me to remain in the solitude of my own room, until the hour of midnight, that I may more fitly prepare for the solemn duties about to be put upon me. Be so kind as to let me know by written word, whether or not, you comply with my request. Your niece,

MINERVA MONSERATE."

In a few moments the octoroon returned, and handed a note to her mistress. The seal was hastily broken, and the senora read:

"BEST OF NIECES:

"You have my full consent to spend the evening as you choose. I wil. excuse you to our guests. I will send you a case of jewels that belonged to your mother. Accept my kindest wishes for your happiness.

"Your ever obliged, UNCLE."

The senora tossed the letter from her, with a contemptuous gesture.

"Nothing else could be done," she murmured, below her breath. Then she turned to her dressing-maid.

"I have obtained permission from my uncle to remain at home, till the expiration of the time set for my wedding. You need not look so strangely, you see I am quite calm about it. Don Carlos will make a noble bridegroom;" the sneer was but half concealed.

"He is not noble; there is nothing noble about him," said the girl, impulsively.

"Well, well, noble or not, you see how the case stands. I am not going down to this party—"

Althea started. "Not going!" she repeated.

"No, I shall stay in the solitude of my chamber, the greater part of the time," returned her mistress.

"And your beautiful ball-dress! Oh, not to wear it at all!"

"You forget I am to be married," said Minerva.

"Yes, but it will not be happy. You look anxious and pale, while you talk about it. Besides, it is mean in them to cajole you into it."

"Hush! Althea, remember you talk about my uncle. By the way, is that sister of yours still alone?"

"All alone," was the answer.

"And would you like to stop with her to-night?"

"What! of all things! to-night! when you need me so much? No, no, no, I can go just as well to-morrow. I shall want something then to take off the heart-ache, because, if you are married, you will go away."

"In any case, I shall go away," replied the young girl. The octoroon watched her mistress narrowly, as she said, "I wish you may carry a happy heart, wherever you go."

"Thank you, Althea. You shall hear from me," murmured the senorita; "good by, and God be with you."

CHAPTER IV

THE SEARCH AND THE ATTACK.

A BEAUTIFUL little supper-room, whose table of Indian letter-wood, is spread for three. Enter Senora Mancha, brilliant in a head-dress, composed of red roses, gold foil, and rich lace. Though her face is sallow, her hair is ebon as midnight, and her manners still those of the Spanish nobility. The Senora moved to the little stand of marble on which stood an apparatus for boiling tea. In a few moments the steam ascended in graceful curves, white as snow-wreaths. Presently, in came the general and Don Carlos. Punctiliously placing himself at the table, the old gentleman motioned for the rest to be seated.

"Yes, yes, I was never more surprised in my life," he said, as if upon some continued subject. "How could she have learned? I am at a loss to know. I think I can trust my sister."

"I *think* you may;" said that lady with no little emphasis.

"I don't care how it was found out, as long as it is known, and she don't object," said Don Carlos, displaying a magnificent diamond ring, as he helped himself to the delicate wafers near; "but the deuce is in it, too. How comes it that she makes no appeal, confesses no disinclination. My dear friend, I fear there's treachery at the bottom. Still, I am vain enough to believe that her playing off was only a girlish whim, for she well knows that I chose her from a legion who would fain be the mistress of my heart, to say nothing of other attractions;" he added with a sly smile.

"I am very glad the thing is settled at last," said the general, with a sigh of relief. "From to-night I cease to hate America."

"Not so fast, my dear friend," spoke up Don Carlos, compressing his lips. "I saw Goreham to-day, radiant in whiskers

and white linen. The presumptuous fool! He was actually
in conference with the governor. We are not quite out of the
woods yet, general. There are vessels going out of the harbor every night—ay! and to-night."

The old Spaniard glanced up, alarmed. He met the wick-
edly smiling eye of his ward.

"I am not in the least concerned," said the latter. "It
takes a great deal to disturb me. The senora's reproaches,
here, even fall upon me with the soothing influence of balmy
showers. If my wife ever has hysterics, I shall study them.'

The general nodded his head approvingly.

"As for El Americano, let him look out for himself, if he
stands in my way, that's all. But I am forgetting my pretty
bird. Senora, oblige me by filling a cup with this charming
tea; and now, thank you—ah! with what a grace it was done!
Now may I ask a very tremendous favor—that you yourself,
with your own fair hands, will take it up to my pretty bird,
with my compliments. Do not be frightened, my guardian,"
he added, as the old senora left the room smiling (for she was
not averse to compliments, even insincere ones), "I have only
put in a little soothing powder; it will affect her volition, and
perhaps her memory. Under ordinary circumstances, it would
but make one sleepy, or more vulgarly speaking, stupid.
She will not appear any the less interesting that she obeys im
plicitly. We shall astonish our guests who do not dream
that they are coming to a wedding."

The general's sister returned with the empty cup.

"How did you find her?" asked Don Carlos, wiping his
mustached mouth, leisurely, with a napkin of exquisite texture.

"Apparently meditating," replied the senora. "She sat
with her prayer-book before her, and seemed much pleased
with the proof of your thoughtfulness."

"Ah! come round at last, like a good child," muttered
the young man; and he opened his cigar case, offered it to the
general, and both strolled out on the open balcony for a
lounge.

Senora Mancha, however, after ringing in the servants to
carry out the table, hurried from room to room to see that all
the arrangements were perfect. Flowers bloomed everywhere,
and fresher was their brilliant beauty, than the cold splendor

of marble statuary grouped here and there. It needed but the flashing of the lighted candelabra to give a bewildering effect to the scene. An hour later and the rooms were revealed in their full magnificence. Soon there was heard the rattle of volantes—by couples came the gay beauties; diamonds, lustrous drapings, bright eyes, nodding plumes, and airy scarfs, with the fluttering of innumerable, gorgeous fans, gave a fairy-like brightness to this vision of Cuban loveliness. Among these throngs, celebrated for their various attractions, moved the elegant Don Carlos, and the stately little general. On this hand and on that, beautiful, eager eyes awaited them, for each was, in Yankee phrase, esteemed a great catch. Many inquiries were made for the Senora Minerva, all of which were skillfully parried or answered. The lady had begged to be excused till a late hour—she would soon make her appearance, etc., etc. Music abounded—the dance went on—the whist-tables were full—singing sounded bird-like, from one of the distant rooms—groups were partaking of ices in another. Suddenly appeared upon the gay, human parterre, Senora Mancha, her yellow face, puckered with wrinkles—her black eyes gleaming a desperate dissatisfaction. Here and there her gay head-dress went bobbing, and more than one remarked that there was trouble somewhere.

"Where was the general? Oh! where was Don Carlos? Had any one seen either of them?"

Yes, the general had been last seen going into the conservatory with a countess, rich and distinguished. Possibly he might be found there. Distractedly Senora Mancha hurried to the conservatory; distractingly she gazed about. No general. Then she plunged into the crowd again—caught a glimpse of Don Carlos, and made straight up to him.

He felt a pull at his coat-sleeve, and looked round frowningly. Dismay fell upon him when he caught sight of the yellow Mancha, working her toothless mouth.

"In the name of all the saints, what is the matter?" he asked.

"Gone, gone," was the muttered response.

"What! who?" exclaimed Don Carlos, who had not the most distant suspicion of the truth.

"Minerva, your bride."

The Cuban started; turned as pale as death.

"Do you mean that she has escaped! Was there not a watch near the chamber?"

"Yes, in the very next room, but she went from the window. The lace curtain is dreadfully torn, one of the best sets, and how I am ever to repair it—"

Don Carlos broke away, white with suppressed feeling. He soon found the general, and electrified him by saying: "Our plans are thwarted, your niece has escaped us. Do you still remain; I will find her—or—" A gleam of fire shot from his wild eyes. The general seemed struck with stupidity.

Instantly a light traveling volante stood at the door. Don Carlos drove rapidly to the custom-house pier. Springing out when arrived there, he sought out the superior officers. They had seen Herman Goreham only two hours before. He had taken passage in the Eagle, an American packet ship. Yes, there was a lady, his cousin. The Cuban showed his teeth at this.

"Then he has missed justice," he hissed. "He was a spy, the tool of the Yankee fillibusters. It had come to his knowledge through papers recently found, a dangerous enemy had been suffered to leave the country. Peace and order were threatened. He had been, this American, the guest of the governor. He had insinuated himself into private confidence; in short, he was a scheming, double-dyed villain." Don Carlos was furious. He frightened the officers thoroughly, and in less than ten minutes a private and concealed guard was posted from the custom-house up along the Paseo, and along the walls to the sea. It happened that Herman had landed but a few moments before, and hurried unsuspectingly along for his carpet-bag. The boat lay concealed in the shadow, and the sailors, idly waiting—two of them Spaniards—heard the conversation of the guards posted on the pier, and drew off silently where they could not be seen. Meanwhile, where was the Eagle? There was no time to be lost. A world of shipping lay in the harbor. The vessels all head into the streets. A belt of thick forest—mast after mast stretching away, and bayward, how close the vessels were! Screw frigates, ships-of-the-line, and no telling which is the Eagle. Don Carlos did not despair, however. A boat was in readiness, and slowly and laboriously it was maneuvered between the unwieldy hulks. He could find no boatmen at hand, and dared not waste time in hunting one up, therefore he seized a pair of oars himself. Just as he passed under the side of a heavy Spanish sloop, a sudden flash, and a heavy weight made his boat rock again. It was the body of some unfortunate sailor, dead, of the fever, and in the moonlight he watched it sliding off with the current. Superstitious, as all Spaniards are, he regarded this event as a poor omen, and bent his energies towards find·'ing the Eagle, with less hope for success than before. Baffled rage tugged at his heart harder than his hands at the oars, and as he glided from stern to stern, and at each attempt met with failure, he cursed his own fate, and particularly cursed Los Americanos.

Meanwhile, the Eagle had been got under way, and was now majestically making for the sea. Don Carlos had missed the sailors in their return to the vessel—had missed his bride and happiness, but it allayed somewhat the irritation of his mind to learn on his arrival on the pier, that Herman Goreham was a prisoner, and in the custom-house ready to be carried to the guard-house. It occurred to Don Carlos that he would, if possible, make the young man a means of conveying the Señora Minerva into his possession again.

Accordingly, he sought him. The young man stood under guard, looking sternly from face to face, as if still mutely questioning his captors.

"So, I see it all," he said, as Don Carlos came into his presence. "Villain, why have you deprived me of my liberty?"

"That shall be shown," said the Cuban, scowling back at him. "It is no crime, I suppose, to steal a young lady from her home—from the arms of her affianced husband, on the very night of her expected wedding."

"Thank God! I have saved her;" said the young man, drawing a long breath.

Don Carlos sprang towards him, his hand under his vest, but in a minute he bethought himself and forced his heated face into calmness.

"Young man," he said, falling back, and commanding his temper under the scornful glance of his rival. "I have the powe to place you in a dungeon where the light of day can

never penetrate—where the walls ooze dampness—where you
will have but the solitary crust and the jug of water—where
your companions will be the worms and the rats, instead of
the birds and the flowers of this beautiful land."

"Very poetical," said Herman, as the Cuban paused a second for breath. The white lips of the latter trembled with
rage, but still he did not let his passion master him.

"Or I can give you liberty," he added.

"That is my right. To-morrow I shall see if a citizen of
America is to be captured for no crime; detained against his
will by a jealous Spaniard."

The Cuban drew a long, deep breath; his eyes glittered—
his fingers worked nervously against his vest.

"You are free if you deliver Senora Minerva into her uncle's custody."

"Impossible. The young lady is by this time on her way
to America. The Eagle sailed at twelve. By consulting your
watch you will find it is somewhat more than a half hour past
that period."

"Perdition!" muttered the Cuban, now growing furious.
"You shall answer for this, fellow—you shall rot in prison,
or be hung as a spy, while I shall leave no means untried to
recover the young lady. For your comfort, know that I shall
take the fastest sailer in port, and it will go hard if, with my
resources, I do not find the niece of General Monserate. Then,
if she be not too much disgraced by your favor, I shall marry
her."

It was Herman's turn to repel now. He sprang like a ti-
ger upon Don Carlos, collared him, and before he could be
reached, shook him till he was black in the face, and flung
him at arms-length almost senseless, and panting on the floor.
At that moment, General Monserate entered. Herman was
struggling in the hold of a powerful soldier. Don Carlos, his
dress in disorder—his hair thrown wildly from side to side, his
face purple and haggard, for the young American had held a
choking grasp, was just rising with the aid of two custom-
house officers, from the floor, covered with dirt, and sheet-
white with passion. Blood had been shed, and Herman was
marched off by the authorities, and thus ended a day that
promised so much happiness at its dawning.

CHAPTER V.

MINERVA ON SHORE.

MINERVA MONSERATE, the young lady left so unexpectedly on board the American vessel, was, as our readers have already seen, the niece of an old Spanish grandee, and consequently of noble descent. We have hinted before, that English and Spanish blood mingled in her veins. Her father had married a young creature, Maria Wells, the daughter of a poor minister of the church of England. Much surprise was manifested at this unequal match, as it was called, but Senor De Monserate, the younger, was by the mere force of his character, as much feared as admired, and when he boldly returned from his travels, bringing his pretty British flower, nobody demurred in his presence, not even the domineering sister, Senora Mancha. The young man seemed very much changed after his marriage—put on the harness of labor, and went to work amassing a fortune. His whole heart and soul seemed absolutely given up to money-making. A child was born—it made little difference; his wife died—there was brief mourning; still he bought and sold, and people began to think there would soon be no end to his wealth. He spent as freely as he made. Though he never indulged in parties, hardly amusements of any kind, he allowed his sister sufficient to cover all such expenses, for in her young days, Senora Mancha was very gay. At last, in the midst of his processes for turning every thing he touched into wealth, he died, but his property possessed such accumulative force, that year by year houses, lands, and ships were added, so that his child was the wealthiest heiress in all Cuba. But of that fact, she was brought up in entire ignorance, as only her uncle, the lawyer who drew up the will, and a very few witnesses knew its conditions. Of this, however, more hereafter.

Minerva had become accustomed to the motion of the ves-

sel which she called her sea-cradle. Though often troubled
with spells of long and deep despondency, yet she endeavored
to keep before her mind the evident certainty of meeting Herman as soon as they landed, or, at all events, shortly after.
Whether she thought the winds would be more favorable to
his voyaging, or that love might guide the helm so that both
vessels should strike shore at the same moment, I know not;
but the fact of the sudden storm having delayed the Eagle,
and indeed put her out of her course, gave her expectations a
more sanguine coloring. On the day before the vessel came
in sight of port, she sat on the deck, her mantle thrown
gracefully over her head so that its folds fell in artistic lines
over her form. She was knitting, while very near her sat the
stewardess, Bandola, reading aloud.

Suddenly the girl paused—the flush of her red blood was
faintly visible under her dark skin.

"How I wish I was white, senorita, and had a lover like
him. Ah! it must be very pleasant."

"Be contented with your lot, Bandola," said Minerva; "the
sweetest rose has thorns, and you might find more sorrow
than joy in the fate you covet. The captain says we shall
sight New York in a day or two," she added, after some moments had elapsed.

"Yes, you have been there before, haven't you?"

"Oh, yes—twice, and each time staid three years. I love
New York dearly, it is a great, glorious place."

"Tell me what you came here for?" pressed the stewardess.

"For my fate," said Minerva, smiling and blushing.

"Your fate," queried the girl, wonderingly.

"No, no; to go to school. Didn't we have splendid times
though, at Madame N—s school? There's where I first saw
him," she added dreamily—then started, remembering who listened.

"Ah! I hope he will be there. What pleasure to see him
standing on shore as the vessel goes in! Oh, I know he'll be
there."

"I hope he will," said Minerva, her bright face clouding, as
a gloomy doubt shadowed her mind.

"But were there no Spanish gentlemen who wanted you to
marry them?"

"Oh, yes," said Minerva, smiling, "one in particular; the richest man in all Cuba."

"And why didn't you?"

"Because I didn't like him—because I detested him," she added passionately.

The shadow grew deeper on her brow; her work fell from her hands. The malignant face of Don Carlos, with its dark, vengeful eyes came before her. What if they had met, Carlos and Herman?—both quick, resolute men. Oh, the sickening apprehension that crept into her heart as the possible result suggested itself. And she alone in the world, poor and dependent, with but the temporary resort to her jewels to keep her from famine. Well, better even that than the wife of that horrible man; better to earn her bread, though how those helpless hands were to accomplish such wonders could not even be imagined.

"There, now you are sad again," said Bandola.

"Yes, I was thinking."

"Why do you think? I never think long enough to make me unhappy. The way to enjoy life, I believe, is to think as seldom as you can."

Minerva made no reply to this sally. A dreadful foreboding had taken complete possession of her mind. She could not sit there in the clear breeze, the pure sunshine—but gathering up her work she went down into her state-room. There, fumbling about the pocket of her traveling dress, she found a little purse, through whose meshes glittered gold.

"Poor, old uncle—he gave me this," she murmured; "he was good, kind, and liberal in all but one thing. Why would he force me, till I had nearly been sacrificed, to marry that dreadful man? What was the fascination Don Carlos exerted over him? I cannot think. Well, at least, I shall have sufficient to pay my passage, and to keep me in some hotel until"—here she paused. She would have added, "until I meet Herman," but her heart fell as heavy as lead when she thought of it. Even the captain's cheerful face and jovial language lacked their pleasant influence for her. She dreaded the sight of the shore, for she had never been so far alone, and now she had none but the captain and poor Bandola to depend upon.

Hearing the step of the former in the cabin, she lifted herself from her painful reverie and went out.

"We shall soon near land," said the captain, cheerily—"but see here, you are looking pale and ill again—I must not have this," and he shook his head.

With great effort Minerva kept back the tears.

"I suppose I must learn to transact my own business," she said, trying to smile, "so I am going to pay you my passage-money." She emptied the contents of her purse upon the table. "There, will you please see if that is enough to cover the expense of my voyage?"

"Tut, tut. Just put that money right back, my dear young lady. I'm the owner of my ship and have no one to consult besides myself—so you'll please oblige me by keeping what little money you have; you will need it all, yourself."

"Oh, I cannot, indeed I cannot be under such an obligation," said Minerva, the quick color coming. "I have other means." She faltered. "You will oblige me infinitely by accepting the passage-money."

"But I tell you my young friend, I fully expect to see Herman Goreham in the city of New York, and he agreed with me for the passage, so I shall settle with him, and you must let me have my way, for I generally do when I set out for it. I'm a very resolute man, you see."

Minerva sat quite perplexed and undecided, The captain lifted the purse and sweeping the gold into it, placed it in her hand.

"And now we must talk a little about the future," he said. "It is possible when you land, our young friend may not be visible. In that case where would you like to go? Have you friends or relatives in New York?"

"Some acquaintances, but no relations. I have made up my mind to go to an hotel."

"I know of an excellent private boarding-house," said the captain; but she exclaimed eagerly—

"Oh, not there—among the many I shall be unnoticed. I prefer an hotel; there I can be alone until I know my fate," she added in a lower tone, and with a quivering lip.

"Just as you please, though it is my opinion that you would be better suited in a pleasant family, but I will not attempt to

dictate, you of course know best. Consult your own inclina
tion, only remember to come to me as a friend in whatever
circumstances of trial you may find yourself."

Two days after that Minerva was driven from the pier to
to the hotel she had chosen. Almost a stranger in a great
city, her heart sank at times, though she strove to think that
Herman would surely come—she should not have to wait but
a little while. But how should she pass the time during that
dreary waiting? Her little room, up many flights of stairs,
had a cheerful look-out, but it grew monotonous to watch the
ever-passing multitude, the same unvarying round of faces.
Her dresses were taken out again and again, but there every
thing was finished, and she dared not array herself in other
than the plainest habiliments for fear of attracting attention.
She little knew how often the question went the rounds, " Who
is that beautiful girl dressed in gray, with the dark, Spanish
eyes?"

One day she had been unusually sad. Captain Wyllies had
been to inform her that as yet he had heard or seen nothing
of Herman Goreham. He seemed, himself, perplexed and unhappy about it, and could no longer make excuses. He had
come to consult with Miss Minerva—would she return to
Cuba? He was nearly ready for the next trip, and he would
see her safely back in the midst of her family.

"Never," was her reply, with a paling cheek. "I shall
never return to Cuba. Captain Wyllies, you will inquire into
this mystery—you will write me whether Herman be alive
or—" she could not speak the word.

"Be assured I will use every means in my power to learn
of his whereabouts. If there has been foul play—mind I say
if—the matter shall be brought to light as far as I have means
and influence. I will not not leave a stone unturned. Meanwhile if you find spies upon your path, you had better avail
yourself of the kindness of a friend of mine, a very estimable
lady, who, if you give her this card, will, for my sake be like
a mother to you. Do not scruple to use my name, or to call
upon me if you are in need."

When he had gone the young girl was more wretched than
ever. She passed the time in writing. Seldom went out, and
for the lack of exercise, began to grow thin and pale.

One day she was inspired with a sudden impulse to walk to the Battery. So arranging herself in her most unostentatious dress, she walked slowly along, her eyes looking straight forward as if she never again expected to see any thing of sufficient interest to attract their glances. The fresh air, blowing cooler as she neared the water, revived her however, and brought a faint color to her cheek. A German band discoursed sweet music, and children in bright dresses running eagerly past her, made her heart beat faster with their happy smiles and cheerful voices. But as she hurried by all these and stood looking at the water, the old desolate, homesick feeling came over her. Only to hear a voice that had once been familiar, how sweet it would be! She sat down upon one of the benches, her pale face bayward, and the past with its happiness and its sorrows came over her in a tumultuous tide. She thought of her school-days—of the pleasant little parties of Saturday night when some of the young students who were well known by the principal, were allowed to mingle socially with the pupils. The bright face of Herman with its blue eyes and gold brown hair, seemed even now beside her as then. How little in those happy days she thought of any coming darkness? The merry girls in their bright dresses, all so eager to receive one smile from Herman, the prince of the college, as he was playfully dubbed, came thronging by. Southern eyes and night black tresses—Northern brows and fair golden hair, but he had turned from all to her. She lived over again the happiness of hearing him call her "beloved"— of listening to his voice that seemed to her of all music the sweetest. Noblest, bravest, most beautiful of all the sons of men he was to her! Then he had followed her to the sunny land of her birth. For two burning summers he had braved the pestilence to be near her. Shudderingly she recalled the first time, that Don Carlos thrust his dark presence between her and happiness—the evil hour when he grew jealous of *El Americano*, and became more impetuous in his suit. His dark hints and wicked insinuations sounded even now in her ears. His black, lurid eyes scorched her soul, and recalled the dreadful repugnance that had been sleeping in her heart since childhood when he was her constant tormentor. And now what had he done with Herman? Had he fulfilled his fright.

ful threats? Did the golden hair lay matted in some foul corner, while the eye, bluer than heaven, sent stony glances after that they could never see? Before she knew it, the round tears were rolling from her eyes, and hearing voices coming that way, she hastily threw down her thick vail and turned her face from the sea. Two young men passed her. She could not forbear one glance, and that sent a thrill of fear through brain and heart. The personage nearest her—tall, straight, and swarthy—was a foreigner. It needed but one glance at his thick, curling mustache and piercing eyes to recognize him. It was Senor Abrates, a Cuban, and boon companion of Don Carlos. Why was he here, following so quickly upon her absence, but as a spy sent by her uncle's ward? The horrible apprehension seized her that she was discovered —that Don Carlos had probably taken the next vessel that sailed after the Eagle, and they were on her track; they would hunt her down as the hound hunts the timid hare. She grew sick and cold at the thought, and gathered her vail in thicker folds. She fancied that the young man half paused as he neared her as if about to speak, and, as she hurried away with trembling limbs it seemed to her that she was followed. After a long, quick walk, however, she ventured to look round. There was no one in sight and she breathed more freely.

11   2

CHAPTER VI.

AN OLD ACQUAINTANCE.

EMERGING into the thoroughfare, she found that the streets were totally unfamiliar to her, and a vague terror was added to her sad anticipations. To be lost in this bewildering city was not one of the least of evils, and to crown her confusion, she could not recall the name of her hotel, or even of the street where it was located. The sudden fright caused by the appearance of a familiar face, had driven every thing else from her mind. Stopping for a moment to collect herself, she took the path that seemed most likely to lead to familiar signs, and hurried on. Street after street she turned, and each seemed farther from her destination. Dizzy, faint, and bewildered, she knew not which way to turn, nor how to ask for directions homeward. Suddenly as she stepped upon a crossing, there was a loud cry—the clattering of horses' hoofs—violent struggling—a hot, moist breath fell on her cheek. She closed her eyes and would have fallen, but some strong arm pulled her again upon the sidewalk. Looking up a moment after, still dizzy and confused, she saw seated in a splendid barouche, two gentlemen and a lady, and in one of the former recognized, and was recognized by Senor Abrates. Before she could move, he was on the pavement by her side, talking volubly in Spanish.

"My dear Senora De Monserate, I am astonished, yet delighted. Did you drop from the clouds that I should meet you just here? Of all unfortunates that I should come near causing so dreadful an accident! Do me the honor to enter my barouche—indeed I must insist; you can not walk, you are very pale."

Really faint as she was with the shock and the excitement, she could invent no excuse.

"My sister; my friend, Senor Velasquez." The introduc

tions were rapid—a pretty face bowed. Some one with a very peculiar and forbidding eye bowed also. Minerva could scarcely take note, for her soul was full of the most dismal apprehensions. They had found her—they would leave no means untried to entrap her. Where should she fly? How escape the doom that seemed awaiting her? Fortunately the name of her hotel recurred to her, and she was driven there.

"May I call!" asked the young man in a low voice, as he handed her out at the door of the hotel; "I have something of importance to communicate."

Like lightning it flashed through her mind that if she made a confidant of this young man, and appealed to his pity, his honor, she might find a surer means of escape from her persecutors. "You may call," was the reply.

Senor Abrates returned to his barouche in high spirits.

"My dear Dora, I mean to make the most of this affair," he said, as he sat with his sister not long after their return, "and I depend a great deal on you to aid me."

"I don't understand you," said his sister, using her fan languidly, and caressing with a little slippered foot, the curly coat of a snowy lap-dog.

"Is it possible you don't know that this senora whom we came near knocking down to-day, is the runaway niece of General Leindres de Monserate? Of course, though as you are fresh from boarding-school, you can know but very little about it."

But the young lady had waked up.

"What! that girl with the plain, plum-colored merino, the greatest heiress in Cuba? How came she here?"

"That's what I'm going to tell you, but you must express no surprise—she has run away."

"But with whom?" The lady was now all attention.

"With no one, unfortunately; or fortunately the gentleman who intended to give her the honor of his company, was arrested on the way. She made her escape. You must know, a friend of mine who confides in me wonderfully, is in love with the girl, and with her fortune, undoubtedly. Now you see, whoever she marries she will richly endow. The field is all clear—why should I not speak for myself?"

"Why, truly? But Manuel, why did not the senor, whoever he is, come and attend to his own business. He is strangely short-sighted," I think.

"The fact is, he was slightly indisposed, and not very slightly either," was the reply. "Between you and me I have a suspicion that *El Americano* tried to throttle him, and nearly succeeded. At any rate I found him in bed just before I came away, bandaged up and quite exhausted. Now, the young lady is a beautiful creature, as you must acknowledge, and it would not be amiss to win her in spite of them all."

"It would be delightful," said the senora, closing her eyes sleepily, yet smiling as she spoke—"to have so rich and handsome a sister-in-law. But it seems to me she has compromised herself somewhat to run away in this romantic fashion."

"Oh, no—under thee ircumstances it is not at all singular, besides great heiresses can do much without provoking the world's scandal. She is an innocent, quiet little thing, I imagine, and yet she has spirit," was the reply. "She is totally without acquaintances, if I judge right, and will be glad of a friend, poor creature. Now you must be that friend. She will confide in you—she will love you, and possibly her lonely heart may reach out to your brother, and with her for a sister you may do what you please, for I am sure she is liberal as well as romantic."

"I wonder if she has many jewels?" mused the senora. Her brother smiled in a sarcastic way.

"Oh, of course; you women never forget your jewels. If a house was on fire, I believe, and you were a mother, the first thought would be the jewels, the next, the child. To be sure she has brought her jewels in anticipation of reverses, may be, and a delightful time you will have of it, comparing heirlooms. I fancy I see you spending hours over the precious treasures. Besides you will suit each other in other respects. She is not long from school—you have just left. What a fund of entertaining conversation there is in store for you ! What a pity I could not be behind the curtain ? I might then hear with what confoundedly poor but particularly clever American gentleman you, too, had fallen in love,"

"You need never be afraid that I shall love a poor man Manuel."

"No, on second thought, I don't know as I need. Your tastes are too much like my own, and you are—pardon me—too lazy to seek a sensation."

To this, the only reply was a small, low laugh.

CHAPTER VII.

THE NEW RESIDENCE.

MINERVA reached her little room quite worn out with excitement, and fell listlessly on the little silken lounge that shared most of her rest. The maid came in with luncheon. She motioned her to set it down, but it remained untasted. Her mind was in a tumult, would it ever be clear again? She addressed herself with all her might to frame a speech, a pretty, pathetic little appeal that might, as novelists say, "melt the stoniest heart;" and by the time the gong sounded for preparation for dinner, she had voted herself successful. To-day, also, she ventured upon a richer garment, and an antique chain of gold and turquoise, of whose value she little dreamed. Hope had awakened in her heavy heart, and touched her face with its charmed hues. She had never looked more beautiful than when she glided to her seat at the long table, and the homage of admiring eyes greeted her, though she was too much preoccupied to notice it.

Glancing up, however, she perceived, fixedly gazing at her with those strange unfathomable orbs, the senor to whom she had been introduced in the barouche. He nodded, she returned the token of recognition, though the matter of meeting him again, gave her uneasiness.

"I thought so," went the rounds of the table; "told you she was Spanish. That gentleman is an Havana planter. A lady of mark, probably, or the contrary. Velasquez has the reputation of a dissipated *roue*."

Meanwhile, Minerva awaited the coming of Don Carlos' friend with some trepidation, and when his card was sent up, could scarcely summon the courage to meet him. He, however, did not seem to notice her nervousness, but began in an off-hand manner to speak of the beauty of the day, and of several little things unimportant in themselves, save as the hinges upon wh ch greater topics hang.

"You have come from Don Carlos," at last Minerva found courage to excl.im, after a pause; "I think that is what you would say."

"I left him 'll," he returned with a peculiar smile; "yes, senora, I have received my orders from him, but it depends altogether upon you, whether I shall execute them."

Minerva look d anxious.

"I prom'sed to serve him to the best of my ability, but it would be doing him an injustice to bring him an unwilling guest."

"Oh! how I thank you!" she exclaimed, sincerely; his meaning was becoming now more apparent. "You would not use unjust measures to force me home again."

"Do I look like such a one?" asked the young man, his brow flushing.

No, indeed he did not; at that moment, self-deceived, animated as he thought by an entirely generous motive, he seemed too noble for treachery. His dark eyes were beautifully sincere, his smile was born of a generous impulse.

Then the "might be," was shadowed forth for a brief season, he had put his real idle self in the background.

"But you must not remain in this isolated situation," he continued. "It will not do in a place where envy and detraction abound. I have taken a suite of rooms for my sister and myself in a private house. We have our own servants, live in fact entirely by ourselves. To ensure success to the plan by which I mean to delude (pardon me, but there is no other way) Don Carlos, my friend, you had better leave so public a place as this. Every day, almost, there are Cubans stopping at the hotels; you would be recognized, and perhaps the victim of some conspiracy."

"What you say is true," said Minerva; "the Senor Velasques to whom you presented me to-day, dined at the *table d'-hote.*"

"He did!" exclaimed Senor Abrates, a frown settling on his face. "Ah! he is a dangerous man, but do not be alarmed, fair lady, I have him under my thumb."

"But, where shall I go?" asked Minerva; the pathos in her countenance transferred to her voice. "I do not wish to be recognized by those I have known before."

"I was about to suggest," continued the young man, "that my sister is very lonely (as I am away much of my time necessarily), and wishes often for a companion. She informed me privately, to-day, that she had fallen in love with you, and that it would be charming if she might prevail upon you to share her society while we remain in New York, which will not be for long. Here is something she has written on the subject."

Minerva took the delicately worded note, her expressive face betraying the pleasure she felt that any one should be so interested in her.

"She is very kind," she said thoughtfully.

"And may I say that you will come?" asked the young man eagerly, gazing at her with new and delighted admiration, which she would hardly have liked had she seen; "there you can live in as strict seclusion as you like, and together, we will, I think, manage Don Carlos."

This last maneuver decided her. It seemed so pleasant to have found friends, real friends; a woman who possibly might understand her; a man who was too noble to recognize the claims of an usurper like Don Carlos.

"Yes, if you think she will not weary of me, I will go."

"Or, rather that you will not weary of her," said Senor Abrates; an exultant fire lighting up his dark eye. "She is the veriest little chatterbox, and will, I think, sometimes, jabber to death."

"If you knew how I desire to have some one talk to me," she said, her fine eyes growing moist as she recalled the long, silent days passed in her little chamber; "you would feel how grateful that chattering you talk of, will be to me. Oh! how I have longed even for a little bird to have beside me, and sing to me sometimes."

"Here is the address, I will leave every thing with you," he said, with instinctive delicacy. "You have only to summon a waiter and order him to call a carriage, then give this direction to the driver, and in fifteen minutes you will find Dora waiting for you, all expectation."

There was an embarrassing pause. Minerva longed to say a word that would lead to some hint of Herman. But she could not. Even the attempted question, whether Don Carlos were very ill, and what was the matter with him, die.. upon her lips. "There will come a time," she thought to herself, struggling to keep up her courage till the last, for the slightest depressing feeling with regard to Herman always set her heart to aching. With a graceful hesitation, Senor Abrates took his leave, and Minerva, somewhat lighter in spirit, went to her room to make preparations.

To her extreme surprise, when she asked for her bill, the charges set down to her, amounted to nearly all the gold she possessed. Unused to regulating expenses of any kind, she had ordered freely, little knowing that even a look or a step must be paid for, especially if the landlord sees indications of wealth in the manners, dress, or habits of the stranger. However, she took the amount from her slender store, then, having attended to her packing, she proceeded as her new friend had directed.

It was with a comparatively light heart that she ascended the marble steps leading to an elegant mansion in the upper part of the city. Within could be heard the singing of a bird, the light, silvery chords of some fairy music-box, while at the nearest window, the richest exotics gleamed temptingly.

No sooner had the servant answered the ring, than coming steps were heard. A beautiful girl attired in a cloud of India muslin, her dark hair coquettishly dressed, the incomparable Spanish fan depending from her wrist, her large eyes, bright with a beaming welcome, came hurriedly from a side-room, and met Minerva with a childlike caress.

"I am so glad you have come," she said, leading her into the apartment she had just left, seating her on a magnificent lounge, and then dropping herself beside her, as if she were a wee girl. "There is Coco, my maid; she will relieve you of your bonnet and mantle. Do you like the music-box? I do, besides, it is so much exertion to play, hark, that is from one of the operas, I forget which, but we will go, you and I, and hear a whole one. I have never been yet, but Manuel has promised, and he is very good. Are you fatigued? Will you go in your room and lie down?"

"If you please, for a few moments," said Minerva, anxious to be alone with her new happiness, for it was a happiness to know again that some one felt an interest in her.

Dora led her into an exquisite little room, hung with draperies of blue silk. It seemed so much like home to be surrounded with these luxuries, that Minerva could have cried for joy like a very child. As it was, a few grateful tears fell quietly, but they were soon chased away by smiles. She lifted the curtain, the window led on a balcony, and looked out on a pleasant yard, bordered with flower-plats, in the midst of a pretty fountain, springing from a shell in the hand of a marble boy, whose bright face shone through the spray with an ever-beaming glance of wondering delight. Not far off, she could see the iron railings of a park, and in the tall trees around her, the birds sang gayly. Here, then, she had found rest; here she could freely tell all her griefs, and lay her plans for the discovery of Herman's fate, for that he was dealt foully by, she never for an instant doubted.

After a few moments of rest, she went again into the room where Dora was. Her new friend lay nestling on a lounge, her eyes closed, the fan hanging listless.

"How graceful she is," thought Minerva, scanning the delicate poise of the limbs, admiring the white, rounded arm. Dora opened her eyes.

"Oh, there you are," she cried gleefully; "I thought you were never coming. Have you rested? Do you never have more color than now? I should think that you had been ill. What pretty hands! do let me see them." Minerva, smiling and pleased, held out her hands for inspection.

"Smaller than mine, I do believe, and what a beautiful ring! Is it an engagement ring?"

Minerva's heightened color answered her, she did not wait for speech, but ran playfully on, amusing her companion vastly more than any thing else could.

"How entertaining she is," was Minerva's second thought, "we shall get along admiringly together."

"Do you play? Yes, charming! and sing, I suppose. So does Manuel, he knew you in Cuba, did he not?"

"Yes, he came sometimes to my uncle's house," was the reply.

"I have heard him talk of you and of a Don Carlos. Pray what kind of a man is Don Carlos? Manuel dislikes him exceedingly, I should think."

"He is pleasant, generally," said Minerva, cautiously; "but he does not make many friends, I believe."

"Here comes Manuel; it must be supper-time."

The young man came in—with graceful self- possession greeted Minerva, and presently the three were seated at an elegant little supper-table, on which glistened a silver service. Scarcely had the meal been tasted when the door-bell rang, and Senor Velasquez was ushered in. Manuel's face said how provoking! and the planter himself apologized with elegant suavity, but seemed none the less inclined to partake with them. His presence destroyed Minerva's pleasure; she was sure the man looked upon her with an evil eye, that he was a spy of Don Carlos; she felt it every time he addressed her with such elaborate politeness. The evening, however, passed pleasantly in spite of his presence. Manuel was a delightful singer, Senor Velasquez played the flute, and even Minerva consented to sing a few little ballads. By the time she retired to rest, the young girl had forgotten her vexatious forebodings, and when Dora, with her childish grace, wound her arms about her neck, and whispered, "Don't you think Manuel sings well," she made the artless reply, "I think your brother does every thing well, my dear friend."

CHAPTER VIII.

HERMAN RELEASED.

Don Carlos stood before a looking-glass. Many were his muttered imprecations as he met the gaze of a disfigured face. His right eye rejoiced in numerous colors beside its original black. A wound upon his cheek had not improved the appearance of his countenance. The Don was dressed in a gay gown, and from his embroidered cap depended a heavy tassel of gold. His dressing-case was a model of luxurious beauty. Bottles chased with silver and gold—little cushions of satiny softness—brushes with handles of ivory—every thing rich, expensive, and rare.

"The scoundrel! he will pay dear for this," muttered Don Carlos as he lifted a cane from its corner and limped out of the room.

"Ah! welcome down-stairs, my dear Carlos," said the old general, rising with alacrity, while at a look from him, withered Mancha, who was embroidering on a bit of yellow satin, brought a light foot-stool for the invalid. "And how are you this morning?"

"A little stiff in the joints," said Don Carlos with a disagreeable laugh. "My good aunt if you would be so kind as to leave guardy and me alone a few moments."

The senora humbly picked up her work and left the room.

"Now my good friend, what have you heard, and what have you been doing?" asked Don Carlos, turning to the general.

"Wonders! wonders!" exclaimed the general, rubbing his hands with intense satisfaction. "The consul has stirred himself in the business, and finds our prisoner guiltless of all conspiracy. My dear fellow, El Americano is to be pardoned instantly on condition of his leaving the country."

"Well," queried Don Carlos, impatiently, in a voice that betrayed that he expected more news of importance.

"Listen; this is my plan. I have bribed Salvetto, the keeper, and he is to have a private carriage at the door of the Jail. There will be two strong men inside with ropes—you understand."

"And they will strangle him,"—cried Don Carlos with fiendish joy.

"Oh, no; not so bad as that. We would not commit murder, my boy, because I am old, and the sin would weigh heavily on my conscience. You have heard me tell of La Vintresse."

Don Carlos nodded his head.

"It was once the most magnificent estate in the environs of Havana. Ah! many a splendid party have I given there, but fire and the cholera, and the hurricane have lent their united rigor to destroy it. You have no idea of the complete desolateness of the place. The walls are demolished—the fields have no boundaries—the water has overflowed, and only a part of the house stands, a melancholy ruin, and a part of the negro quarters. In this last, there is a strong room which on the plantation I used as a jail. Ah! you begin to understand. The prospect looks out upon a few stunted palm-trees, the distant hills, and an arid plain. There is not a creature living within a mile, and nobody passes there, for the place has the reputation of being haunted. It is haunted by the spirit of desolation. There is where, at night, I shall have this insulting American conveyed, and he shall learn that he can not annoy a gentleman with impunity here, as in his own land. Old Jose who is cruel enough for any duty, shall live there and take care of him. Jose has a love for the old place, and is just lazy enough to covet such a life. He was born at La Vintresse, and I have had a room prepared for him. A dreary time it will be for El Americano. He will have no books, no papers, no amusement, little exercise; in fine, he will probably go mad, for I shall take an opportunity to supply him with news, and of no very cheerful kind."

"Guardian, that is a magnificent plan and worthy of your genius," cried Don Carlos, his green and black eyes kindling. "But," his face grew grave again—"we are no nearer to finding Senora Minerva. She has escaped us. Signor Abrates writes me nothing encouraging."

"Have no fear on that score—we shall find her. But I tell you it will not do to trust to others; we must go for curselves."

"Do not I know that?" cried the Cuban vehemently. "Should I not have been there ere this, but for the vile clutches of that Yankee?"

"Patience, patience," said the general, "you will go there yet. You are nearly well. A sea-voyage will refresh you, and fully repair all damages. I have engaged our passage."

"What!" Don Carlos started from his chair—"and I this figure?"

"I tell you, you will be well enough by the time we land in New York. We will set out immediately to Saratoga, and it will go hard with me but we will find her."

"To Saratoga!—Zounds! no, not there, above all places."

"I tell you, yes; here is a letter found in the pocket of that intriguing Yankee; it is directed to his parents who, I should presume, are vulgar farming-people in that same village of Saratoga. What more likely than that she should be found there? Once let me get her in my possession—the renegade child. I'll teach her that she can not lose old friends so readily."

Don Carlos mused. "There is something in that," he said "She may have known of the fact that his people lived there."

"To be sure, and there's where she is, snug and cozy, setting them wild about him. We will make their ears burn, my Don! We will make her glad to gain once more the protection of a home. As soon as the sun sets, Jose will be here with the carriage. Our volante will also be ready and we can drive immediately after to the Grand Careel."

The evening was dark and the streets of Havana illy lighted or not at all. It was late into night when the general and his ward took their seats in the volante, and were driven rapidly after the clumsy carriage that was to convey the prisoner from his dreary confinement to one as much more cruel as it was monotonous. The great building loomed up darkly, standing near the foot of the Punta. Palace-like it reared its regal front, and the dim starlight made it an imposing object. At that moment, Herman Goreham stood at the grated window of his cell looking forth and longing for liberty. In the two months and more of his confinement, he had changed from the self-reliant, dignified man, to the pale, bowed-down captive. His cheek was thin, his beard and hair were grown, and in his eye glittered the restlessness of his soul. Captivity was not his only nor his greatest trouble—he mourned over the unknown fate of Minerva. His efforts to see the captain of the Eagle had all been fruitless. Some unseen influence outside his prison-walls, with more money and more power than he, was working him injury. He had attempted to obtain justice by sending a statement of his case to the American cousul, but whether it had reached him he did not know. He had been able in this loathsome place, where punishment was regulated by the ability of the prisoners, to obtain a better apartment than the common cells where the sights he saw and the sounds he heard, offended his moral nature. But he was by no means placed in congenial society. His room-mates were, a military man who spent his hours in cursing and gaming, and a planter incarcerated for some political offence, who joined his comrade heart and soul in these elevating amusements. The room was large but not over cleanly. Great webs, black with age and dust, dangled from the cornices. The walls were disfigured with rude drawings and ruder scrawls, in Spanish poetry. The floor was dirty and the ceiling obscure. The two prisoners were men of forbidding exterior, who when they found Herman averse to joining in their immoral practices, assailed h.m with vituperation albeit it was guarded by eloquent and elegant Spanish. He understood it all, for though unable to converse with fluency in the language, he could read it and translate with ease.

To-night the image of Minerva had been more than usually present and distinct. He had fretted himself nearly into a fever in his vain attempts to imagine what she possibly might do, or where go. In the captain of the Eagle he had unbounded confidence—he knew that she would be placed in a good home. But what if, feeling her lonely and unprotected state, she should return? The thought gave him anguish. Suppose she was already the wife of that intriguing Cuban? It was horror to think. He tried to shut all such images from his mind, but they would return with redoubled

vividness. He walked back and forth rapidly, and envied the
two sleepers who had thrown themselves upon their cloaks
and snored soundly.

Suddenly he heard the key turn in the lock of his cell door.
A jailer entered with a *capitan de partido*, or local magistrate.
The former held a small paper lantern in his hand and moved
with a slow step, as if in the capacity he was, he desired not
to be the bearer of good news.

The man came forward with his usual greeting, "Do you
confess your fault?"

"I have nothing to confess," was the answer.

"It makes no difference," replied the jailer, calmly—"you
are at liberty. A carriage awaits you at the door."

"At liberty!" Charmed words—the young man's face
brightened—he straightened himself. "At liberty!" he repeated incredulously.

"You will walk this way if you please, senor," said the
man.

Herman followed incredulously. He took down his hat,
his linen oversack, and put them on as one in a dream. He
moved out into the great black passage-way and felt the wind
from the sea strike damp against his forehead. The jailer
held up his lamp in the wide entrance. It flashed full in the
faces of the general and Don Carlos;—evil omen! For a moment Herman drew back—he feared conspiracy, else why
those two of all men, and here at such an hour, close upon
midnight? The carriage stood just beyond.

"You are to go immediately from the country, senor," said
the jailer.

"Am I to be driven to the pier?" asked Herman.

"I know nothing about it, senor, except that by order of
the consul you are at liberty," was the reply, somewhat impatiently.

Herman drew a long breath and stepped out. The carriage door was flung open. He hesitated—placed his foot
upon the step—there was a scuffling noise. His worst fears
were verified—he was a prisoner gagged and bound

Don Carlos and the general laughed out loud and long,
then drove home to confer together.

CHAPTER IX.

A NEW EXPERIENCE.

IT was settled that the general, his sister, and ward, were to travel with any number of servants, and any amount of luggage. The decision threw Senora Mancha into alternate ecstasies of rapture and despair. Rapture, for the general gave her an unlimited purse; despair, that she was old, and not quite capable of playing the coquette, as it had been her pride and pleasure to do in former years. However, she could display her wardrobe, and kill somebody with envy if she could. Such head-dresses as she meant to have! and such fabrics for dresses; above all, such variety! She could have not only ninety-nine, but the hundredth, and she began counting up the needed trunks, and sending for more. Very gracious she was to Althea, Minerva's dressing-maid, for the girl could fit and make dresses to a charm, even upon her withered figure.

"I'll tell you, what, Althea," said the old senora, sitting in her rocking-chair, and languidly fanning; "I didn't think of it, but if you'll try your best to please me, I will take you to the American Saratoga."

"What! and shall I see my mistress?" asked the girl. "Oh! that will be delightful."

The senora's brow clouded. Minerva had never been a favorite with her, for she inherited some English tastes and traits, one of which was absolute truth-telling, and nothing troubles the old and vain so much.

"It is no treat to me," she said, "to expect to meet her; the girl has disgraced herself and us. I care not if I never see her again."

"She will find friends enough," said the octoroon, musingly; "everybody admired her. Do you think if she came back, Don Carlos would marry her?"

"I don't know; all I can say is, that I would not, if I were him," said the Mancha, shortly.

"Nor I him, if I were her," muttered Althea.

"What is that? No insolence, miss," cried the old vigaro her black eyes flashing.

"You should not speak so sharply," said the girl, giving a short, impatient movement. "I don't know but I have ruined this sleeve, you startled me so."

"Well, well; I will be more careful," replied the old woman, anxiously, surveying the threatened trouble. "Remember that is something I cannot match; I would not have it spoiled for the world. But as for Senora Minerva, she is a very graceless girl. Only think of it, to run away—to bring scandal upon a family like ours. I shall not be unhappy if we never see her again, though the general will leave no means untried to find her."

While the senora and the dressing-maid were talking thus, Minerva was unwillingly arraying herself for the opera. Dora had urged her into compliance with her request that she would accompany her there. But, though yielding, and taking no little pains to disguise herself, she was very unwilling to go. She had been already three times, and on each occasion her pleasure had been damped by the presence of Senor Velasquez, whose bearing had gradually assumed the complexion of an ardent admiration. His attentions were not only annoying to Minerva, but Senor Abrates looked upon him with a lowering brow, and began in attitude at least to question his motives. On this particular night, Senor Velasquez was seen as usual, moving toward the box where Dora and Minerva were seated. Manuel cast an inquiring glance toward his *protege*. Her face was clouded by anxiety.

"I wish he would not come," broke impulsively from her lips; "he annoys me."

"You shall not be troubled by his attentions; I will speak to him—there is no other way." A moment after Senor Abrates came back, pale and much excited, while Senor Velasquez was nowhere to be seen.

During the evening the young man devoted himself more closely to Minerva than ever before. He seemed to watch her every motion, and anticipate her slightest wish. This was not wholly agreeable to her. There was not a spice of coquetry in her nature, and consequently any attentions of such a character from one for whom she had no answering emotions were in a high degree repulsive. At the close of the entertainment, he applied himself with assiduity to assist her, in fact, he confused her by the closeness of his attention, and this confusion was by him attributed to a possibly growing tenderness for himself. Minerva had on one or two occasions been somewhat surprised by his demeanor toward her, now there was no mistaking his manner, and it gave her heart a new and regretful pang. The next day and the next, his gentleness of manner remained and increased. Manuel was often in the house, he seemed to find his greatest pleasure in sitting beside Minerva, in listening while she sang, in doing any little trivial service for her, in his mute but expressive admiration. Dora seemed also to feel a great sympathy for her brother. She was always telling of his goodness, his little points of amiability, and sometimes she left them alone together. Thus, the poor girl's situation was becoming every day more unpleasant. Not even the gilding about her pretty cage, the luxuries, Dora's little affectionate ways, could compensate for this miserable certainty, for a certainty it speedily became. At last, Manuel declared his love in the most passionate language, and entreated her to become his wife. In no other way, he protested would she be longer safe, for Senor Velasquez had set sail for Cuba, and would probably before long meet Don Carlos, and then his search would be indefatigable. His sister came to his help. Tears and smiles were tried, great offers, and patient persistence. At last, Minerva compromised. They must give her a week to decide, by that time she should have fully made up her mind. Under this arrangement, she was to be entirely free for a short space, and it was a relief to have gained that advantage. Dora, meantime, used her liberty. She had made some new acquaintances, and finding that her once pleasant companion had grown somber, and even dull, she did not covet so much the pleasure of her society. The freedom of American ladies was charming to her, she had learned to move upon the public promenade with as careless a mien as any of them, and liked the pleasure, dear to every Cuban, of being looked at and admired. Meanwhile, Minerva was left much to herself. There was but one alternative, to accept the offer of Senor Abrates, or leave the house. Never once did she think of returning to Havana, there to throw herself upon the protection of her family. "Never," she declared, when the thought presented itself, she would die first. But what was she to do? Where to go? Anywhere to get from the haunting presence that now troubled her, from the belief that she was being watched, haunted, and might at any time be discovered and forcibly returned. She examined her little store, it was very small, barely possible to procure her board in a private way for a few weeks. But there were her jewels, they could be pawned, she shuddered at the thought, should she ever come to that. Yes, it would be better than the miserable suspense in which she was living. Besides, she could depend much on the friendship of Captain Wyllies, he had told her to come to him if she were in trouble, and it was almost the fifteenth of the month, the time his vessel was due. It remained to be decided how she should leave the house. She determined on taking only a large valise, packing it with the most important of her clothing, and secreting her jewelry within. Then she engaged a coachman, and having given him directions, she took her departure on a day when neither Manuel nor his sister were expected to be at home till the evening. Directing to be driven to a street which she had ascertained was at the extreme end of the city, and near the shipping, where she was sure she could hear from the Eagle, she was accordingly set down before a small, neat house, whose very minute sign told that boarders were taken there. A very civil woman answered her knock, and she was ushered into a small parlor, well filled with old furniture, and smelling of the cooking, the odor of which came from the kitchen near by. Minerva gave her name as Angeline Smith, and after the first preliminaries, was ushered into a narrow, low ceiled chamber, which she was to consider hers while she could pay for it. It was with a feeling of relief she heard that the landlady knew Captain Wyllies well, he had staid there sometimes, and recommended his mates, as it was a genteel boarding-house, she added, laying great stress upon the word that betrayed her self-respect.

Here was a new phase of life, the Cuban heiress installed

in Mrs. Brown's boarding-house, under the assumed name
of Smith, nothing to do, only painful memory for a com
panion.

"It seems to me she's of the solitary sort," Mrs. Brown
would say; "she just speaks to nobody, though I can'
think it's because she considers herself superior. But isn'
she a beauty? and it's my mind, that she's seen better days."

Meanwhile, Minerva patiently waited for the captain's re
turn. The fourteenth passed and the fifteenth, still no tidings
The sixteenth brought Mrs. Brown to Minerva's door, with ar
ominously long face. Behind her were heard sobs, it was the
good Bandola, and alas! she brought sad news; the captain
had died two days out, of yellow fever, and was buried in
the ocean. Minerva felt her heart sink, this was worse than
all the rest; she had now no real friend. She took Bandola
into her little room, and the two mourned and wept together.
The poor girl did not know what she should do now, she
said, sobbingly, that she never should find so good a master
again, and, oh! how cruel it seemed to throw him into the
water, he who had been so kind to her! She had, she further
said, engaged to go still as stewardess on the same vessel, but
that was different from what things would have been if the
captain had lived.

"And I too, must do something, Bandola," said Minerva,
mournfully. "I have but a very little money left, and where
am I to get more?"

"Then you have heard nothing from your home," said
Bandola, with a look of significance.

"Nothing, it is wearing me out," responded Minerva. "If
I could only hear the worst," she added, with a grieving lip.

"You would not go back—why not, and find what you
wish to know? It would be delightful to have you in the
vessel."

Minerva shook her head.

"It is of no use, I can not go back; but I must do something," she added, with energy, "something to forget. I can
not live in this manner, it is killing me."

"What can you do?" murmured Bandola, with sorrowful
sympathy.

"I can at least write to the consul at Havana, I wonder I

have never thought of it before. He will make inquiries for me, and at the same time keep my letter strictly private. I will write immediately. When do you sail, Bandola?"

"In a week," the girl replied. "I can get your letter safely to the consul. I have seen him, he came on board once, before our last trip, with a little, dark Spanish gentleman, the captain called General."

"The consul, you are sure, came with *him?*" cried Minerva, breathlessly. "Could it have been my uncle, General Monserrate? Then they were on some business connected with *him*, with Herman. Do you know what they came for? what did they do? how act? tell me."

"I can only tell you that they went into the cabin, and I saw nothing more of them till they came out again. I heard this old man say, 'then it is settled, you will take him;' and he answered, that he would. When we sailed, the captain was very anxious, and delayed as long as he could. I thought he was waiting for somebody, but he must have been sick then, for he was irritable and would not say much, only that 'twas no use waiting any longer, and something about the second time."

"Then, Bandola, it was about Herman, I am sure—oh! this suspense, it is terrible, what could have happened? Yes, those words, 'it is the second time,' confirm my fears, yet, what, alas! can I do but wait?"

"I wish I could help you," said the stewardess.

"You can not," replied Minerva. "I must help myself."

Bandola had been gone but a few moments, when the hostess came up to say that a gentleman had called, and wished to see her. This announcement threw her into a tremor of apprehension. It was impossible, she said, to see any one, she was ill, she must be excused, at all events. What if it should be Abrates! He would leave no means untried to trace her.

Back came the little woman again, her voice in a tremor, to say that the gentleman said he *must* see her, as his mission was urgent, and most important.

"What is he like?" asked Minerva, in a way that made the hostess look at her suspiciously.

"A tall man, I can not say, who like," she answered, "his

face is in the shadow, and he don't look up, but I am sure it is of great importance, as the gentleman says."

"I can not go," cried Minerva, with decision. "Oh! suppose it should be Don Carlos himself?"

"Don Carlos," murmured the woman, wonderingly, and with another of her peculiar glances, "a foreign gentleman, then I thought as much."

The poor girl knew not what step to take next, she seemed to be environed with difficulties, turn which way she would, there was trouble in store for her. Neither did she like the manner of her hostess at times. Was it possible she suspected her integrity?

"I will tell you a little of my history," she said in a low, rapid voice. "I am a foreigner, and I have left relatives who oppressed me, who did not use me well. Of these I am mortally afraid, and I thought it might be, the man below stairs was one of them. I know not what to do. I must go, I suppose, but I wish to ask as a favor, that you will go with me, and remain in the room."

The woman assented, and trembling like a leaf, Minerva descended the stairs. She took a step into the room, and then remained, almost transfixed, for before her stood none other than Senor Velasquez, the same cold smile on his lip, the same deep cunning in his eye, vail it as he would with his long, sweeping lashes.

Her next movement was one of dismay, as he came cautiously toward her, and held out his hand. He frowned a little, but spoke nevertheless in his ominously soft voice.

"I am happy to see you, senorita."

"I—I thought you had sailed for Cuba," faltered Minerva.

"Such was my intention, senora, but I delayed the voyage, thinking I might be of some service to you. Have you a message, senora? If so, allow me to be the bearer."

"How did you find me here? and why have you come?" exclaimed Minerva, her vexation getting the better of her prudence.

"I found you easily, senora, I had only to follow the dictation of my heart. I came, thinking that I might do you a favor. Can I see you alone, for a few moments?" he asked, in Spanish, looking askance at the woman beside them.

"If you will allow it, I prefer she shall remain," replied Minerva, in the same language. The man frowned, but seemed to comply with the best grace he could assume. He then spoke again in Spanish, told her of Don Carlos' determination to seek her, of his unalterable decision to wed her, and ended with the declaration that unless she placed herself beyond his power, he would certainly find the means to possess her.

"But, what shall I do ?" exclaimed Minerva, frightened and pale to the shade of death.

"Senora, I love you, I am well connected, I am rich, make me happy ; as your lawful defender, you shall then have nothing to fear."

"O Heaven, pity me !" cried Minerva, aghast. "Senor Velasquez, I can not think why you have come thus to terrify and insult me. You know my circumstances, you should pity and protect me ; it is cruel in you."

"I offer to protect you," he said, his voice passion-smothered, "there is no other way, you are young, lovely, and alone. To what scandal are you not subjected ? Besides, there is a tie between Don Carlos and myself, we are both sworn brothers in a secret league. Unless you are my wife—" he made a long pause, "there is no safety for you. I am bound by an oath."

Minerva fell back a pace or two, then her strength leaving her, she sank upon a lounge near.

"Persecute and destroy me, if you will," she said, at last, her voice husky with terror, "but never speak a word of love to me again. I will not hear it, you have my final answer." The proud lineage spoke then in the firm lip, just curved by scorn, in the flash of the eye, the swell of the nostril.

"Senora, you invite your fate," he said, in his smooth voice but his eyes glittered with illy restrained passion. "I have striven to avert, but I can do so no longer. Let me further tell you, that you can not hide from me, with all your woman's ingenuity. I could penetrate through any and every disguise, it is not new work for me."

"No, I judge not," cried Minerva, her scorn taking words ; "your honor has doubtless been compromised more than once in a similar business. I read that in your face from the first.

There is no need for any further conversation, allow me to
bid you good night."

"Stop, senora," exclaimed the man, his whole frame rigid
with the effort to suppress the fiery tempest that raged in his
veins. "I do not often stop to plead even of women, but I
do implore you to consider for a few moments—for a second
only, the consequences of your arrestage—I can use no other
word—by Don Carlos. Your determination to resist his powerful influence—and it is more powerful than you know—may
involve the liberty and even the life of others, of one other,
certainly. Do not be rash, senora; do not throw all protection off; I would not have you think me utterly selfish—
Heaven knows that my feelings are purely honorable. You
must still let me be your friend, your counselor. It may be
that my influence will be of some avail; you are impetuous,
and too easily offended. What have you ever seen in me
worthy of your rash judgement but now."

What had she seen? she questioned herself! Surely nothing. An unaccountable, perhaps rash impulse, had prompted
and possessed her. Why should she make an implacable enemy of the man? Doubtless he might still be her friend.
And there was a hidden meaning in what he had said.

"Perhaps I have been needlessly severe," she said, her manner softening, "you do not know to what persecutions I
have been subjected. I wish indeed I had a friend." The
tears came in her eyes—her lips trembled—never had she appeared so lovely.

"I pledge you my honor, I will be that friend," he said in a
voice of apparent sincerity. For a moment she trusted him,
and had she not looked in his eyes, she could have accepted
his proffered kindness with alacrity—but there was something
there that chilled her. She only said, "I thank you;" allowed him to take her hand for a parting pressure, and she
was alone, dreading, trembling, and bewildered.

"Oh! what shall I do?" she cried in anguish.

"My poor child," said the landlady, much affected, "how
can I help you?"

' Dress me as a servant—put me into somebody's kitchen
—only disguise me so that I can never be recognized—it would
be the greatest favor."

"You go in a kitchen," murmured the woman, smiling and glancing from head to foot as she spoke.

"Yes, let me discolor myself—stain my face—cut off my hair —any thing for safety. My uncle is a powerful man and a rich man. Don Carlos, oh! he is terrible, and he is determined to marry me;" she shut her eyes shuddering.

"But had you nobody to go to? No friends who would not see you wronged?" queried the landlady.

"None, none,"—was the reply. "I am an orphan—my father had but one brother—my mother neither brother nor sister. I am utterly alone. Don Carlos has always been my tyrant. When I was a little child he cut off all my hair because I resisted his petty rule. He has always been so—I dread his love and his hate. Both are combined in his regard toward me. Out of revenge he will hunt me, and what other motive he can have now I know not—but it must be a powerful one to bind him with my uncle in so close a compact."

The good, honest Mrs. Brown did not quite comprehend the distracted language and manner of her new acquisition, but her motherly heart felt that she was in deep trouble. In all her affliction, her first thought had been—her first call, for a minister—so she said now—

"Shan't I call in Parson Edmunds? He knows what to say to people that are in affliction, and he prays that fervent that you hold your breath—I do, for it seems as if he was almost in heaven, and right near to God himself. It might relieve your mind wonderful to hear him."

With her present instinctive dread of new faces, Minerva shrank from seeing a stranger.

"No, if you please, Mrs. Brown, let me be alone. And pray admit no one but Bandola. If I had dreamed that man was in America, I should have put myself more on my guard —I should have confided in you. How did you know he wished to see me? Did he not ask for another name?"

"Yes, but he described you—he said he knew it was you. I was impressed that perhaps it was some one related to you."

"You could not have been expected to do differently under the circumstances," said Minerva. "I must try in some way to avoid him. When Bandola comes again we will confer together."

CHAPTER X

ANOTHER DISGUISE.

THE next day the stewardess visited Minerva. For a long time they consulted, and it was finally agreed that Bandola was to find some out-of-the-way place, where she could rent and furnish a small room, and Minerva was to disguise herself as thoroughly as possible. For this purpose Bandola was sent to a store where second-hand clothing was sold, to select what would best suit her purpose. She returned with a plain gingham frock, a long apron, a frilled cap, and a false front of grizzled hair. "There, your own father wouldn't know you," cried the girl, clapping her hands at the transformation. "You must only try to look old, and make some lines on your forehead. I have found you a room," she went on to say, "and I shall furnish it to-morrow. I told the man it was for a poor widow lady, who would stay for a few weeks till she went away to her relations, and so you know how to act. You can pretend to sew all the time, and when I come back I will board with you. I must lay in a supply of goods so that you may not go on the street much, but even then, you could change your walk and go bent over, so that nobody would know."

"You have laid out quite a programme for me," said Minerva, grateful for so much and so timely assistance. "Let us put it immediately into action. I long to be away from here. But first, my jewels must be turned into money. Will you go to a pawnbroker for me and get them taken care of, for as long a time as possible. I may be able to to redeem them. And now for my letter," she added, as Bandola received the package, consenting cheerfully.

At last, with great caution and secrecy, Minerva was installed in her humble lodgings. The metamorphosis was complete. A cap and large-bowed spectacles, a front of lighter

hair than her own, and the anxious expression that care and
trouble had given her, made her seem in reality thirty years
older. Her jewels had brought her ten pounds—they should
have realized a hundred, but Bandola was ignorant of their
value, and the broker was an unscrupulous rogue. With fifty
dollars, however, and the little she had remaining from her
former store, Minerva felt comparatively easy in regard to the
future—for some weeks at least. She depended upon the
news that Bandola might bring her. The latter was to find
her way to the consul's to deliver the letter into his very
hands, and to intimate the extreme caution that was needful
in the case.

For the first time, Minerva felt comparatively at ease. She
was certain of having escaped the notice of Senor Velasquez,
and as for Senor Abrates, she did not fear that he could attempt to look her up—he was not the kind of man to put himself to much inconvenience, even in a case involving the most
important consequences.

This case was not to continue long, however. Weeks
passed, and there was no news from the Eagle. Every day
Minerva procured the paper, and at last, after a fortnight's de-
lay beyond the usual time, she saw her name in the list of ar-
rivals. Now her heart beat gladly—Bandola would come—
was even then, perhaps on her way, and she hummed merrily
over her work, save at times when the thought that perhaps
the girl might be the bearer of sorrowful tidings, gloomed her
face and saddened her spirits again. Day after day passed,
however, and Bandola came not. In sickening anxiety, Minerva watched and waited, seated at the little window that
overlooked the narrow street, and afforded a glimpse of the
harbor. At last she resolved to run the risk of a visit to the
vessel. It was not far off, and any change was better than
this harrowing dread. Attiring herself in her street disguise,
she passed along by the buildings whose doorways were filled
with noisy children, and skirted rapidly the long, narrow pas-
sage-ways so full of bales and trucks, and busy workmen, till
she reached the wharf. The first sight that greeted her eyes
was the ensign of the vessel of which she was in search. Eagerly pressing forward, regardless of the dangers she ran in so
crowded a locality, she soon gained the plank that was placed

from the shore to the vessel's side, and with eager steps and a
beating heart, inquired of the first man she saw, who proved
to be the steward, for the captain.

" He's ashore, maam," was the answer, civilly given; " won't
be here till to-night at ten."

" I wished to inquire for some one," said Minerva, as the
man made a motion to go on, " if the stewardess is on board
—she is a friend of mine. Can I see her?"

The man stopped instantly at this, and a change came over
his face. He was a slightly built German, of a very fine complexion and handsome countenance, and Minerva had noticed
more than once on her former voyage that he took an unusual
interest in the pretty stewardess. Now he regarded the
speaker narrowly, before he replied in a lower voice—

" Bandola, we do not know what has become of her."

" Not know what has become of her?" repeated Minerva,
slowly and in extreme surprise.

" No, madam—you are a friend of hers, perhaps you will be
interested to hear. If you will please take a seat in the cabin,
in a moment or two I will be at liberty."

Minerva went slowly down the steps leading into the cabin.
It did not seem the same now that it knew no longer the be-
nign presence of Captain Wyllies. How overwhelmingly the
past came to her memory! There was the state-room taken
by Herman yet never claimed. How mournfully empty it
seemed! The recollection of that first morning at sea rushed
across her mind with dizzing force. How had she survived
the knowledge that she was alone, and deserted—going a
stranger to a comparatively strange land? Now in the short
space that had intervened, the good captain had gone—Herman was lost to her and Bandola missing. The steward came
in in the midst of her painful reflections.

" I don't know what to tell you of Bandola," he said.
" She was always free to leave the vessel, and always returned
in safety. But this time we waited there, four hours, but no
Bandola. She went away as usual, and said she should be
back in time for dinner, but she was not. I did not grow un
easy, however, till four o'clock; then I thought she ought to be
on board, and I went to look for her. She had two or three
friends. I knew them and went to their houses. They had

not seen her. Then I walked till dark in the hopes of meeting her. No, she could not be seen, and I wondered what it meant. There was no good in looking, however. I must hurry back to see to supper. After tea I sent the cook one way, and I took another—no Bandola anywhere. The next day we looked and inquired, but in vain. Well, so we waited and waited, I running everywhere—though to no use, until I give her up—no use!"

An emphatic gesture accompanied the last word.

"But can you think of nothing—no reason why she went? Did she say any thing with reference to a lady who came passenger in this vessel four months ago, a Cuban lady?"

"Oh! yes, plenty," cried the steward, eagerly. "She told me she had seen her, and had some business to transact for her. There was a reward offered to every man on board this ship, and her too if we would find a clue to that lady. Ah! Bandola was an honorable girl. It would have made her rich, and she knew all the time, but would not tell. Very honorable!" and the young man shook his head and sighed while his face took on a profound sorrow.

Minerva was plunged again in doubt and despondency. The plot had not ceased working yet—her uncle had not given her up. She more than suspected that Bandola had been watched and tampered with, for she was certain the girl would never have abandoned her cause. New fears for her fate were now added to her perplexing trials—new and terrible anxieties. She arose to go—her heart was too full of grief to say more, though more than one question was on her lips.

"I am sorry," she articulated—"I am very sorry. I hope and trust she may be found."

"It is strange," responded the steward, who followed politely—"but we shall try again—I don't despair wholly, of finding her."

Minerva was on the point of leaving the vessel when a voice arrested her. It inquired for Captain Denver, the master of the ship. Minerva dared scarcely raise her eyes, but her extreme fright forced her to the effort. As she knew before, it was Senor Abrates, looking miserably pale and woe-begone. Evidently he was on the search for her. For a moment, Minerva felt a dizzy faintness, but her effort at self-command was effectual. Senor Abrates did not notice her even by a glance The thread-bare shawl, and antiquated bonnet, made no demands upon his fashionable attention. He passed on by her, as if utterly unconscious of her presence, and she hurried from the ship, anxious only to regain her solitude and relieve her full heart by bitter-tears. She had nearly reached the street where her lodgings were, all the time dimly conscious of following footsteps—but her mind was so filled with her trouble that she did not stop to ask if any new danger threatened. She was now on the door-step, her hand touching the rusted latch of the wooden entrance, when suddenly her whole soul grew dark as if some awful shadow had enveloped it in densest gloom. The footsteps had ceased. Too much frightened to look, she yet felt that there was a presence beside her, and darting into the house, she did not pause till safely within her own chamber and the lock secured, she threw herself breathless and trembling upon her low bed. After some moments had elapsed, she went cautiously to the window and looked out. Her impressions had not deceived her. Standing motionless on the opposite side of the street was a tall figure, enveloped in a cloak which he handled gracefully as only a Spaniard can. At that moment he was turning away, annoyed it might have been by the fixed stare of a group of children, who in their turn had constituted themselves a body-guard of gazers, whose impertinence equaled his own. Minerva knew then that Senor Velasquez had found her out in spite of her disguise. Indignation fired her blood—her passion made her walk the floor fiercely with clenched hands, and the often reiterated exclamation—"He shall not insult me thus! What right has he to invade my privacy? I will not be known—I defy him—I defy them all—I will outwit them all."

It occurred to her then to form some other plan, and she sat down to deliberate. Her money she always carried with her, save a little placed away in case of emergency. She essayed to take it from her pocket. Where was her pocket? She surely had it when she went out—it was gone. Looking more closely she perceived that it had been skillfully cut away —the cup of her trouble had received the one drop more. A theif had abstracted it and she was nearly penniless. No words can express the blank misery with which this new and aggravating trouble filled the mind of the friendless girl. Without money what could she do? Where go? None to apply to, save those whose interested motives she could not fathom. Fortunately she remembered that she had paid nearly a month's rent in advance, so that at least she should not be turned out upon the street, homeless and houseless. But the prospect before her was, oh! how dreary! Her supply of necessary food was exceedingly limited—she had been intending to replenish the meager store, but had put it off from day to day, and now it would take nearly all she possessed to refit her larder. That night, after dark, she stole out for a few moments and bought her provisions, determined to keep herself in strict seclusion, and preserve her incognito at all risks.

CHAPTER XI.

THE HOME OF FARMER GOREHAM.

A plain, white farm-house, nestling down amid trees of a century's growth, surrounded by noble orchards and fields, whose grassy billows were always in gentle unrest, overlooking a sparkling trout stream; in the rear the solid granite hills, with here and there silver tubes of water laid along their rough sides. Such was the home of old Farmer Goreham, or, as he was better known, honest old Ben.

Nothing was wanting to complete the picturesque effect of this woodland home scene. The well, with its gray mosses mingling with brown, and its high-curved sweep was there; the garden, with its borders of lilacs and roses; its full-seeded sunflowers, browning in the summer heat; its crowing hens, and brooding chickens; its bright array of milk pans and cans, its great white and black dog, in leather collar, stretched along, his bushy head on his right forepaw, and the eyes looking up now and then with almost human intelligence; the long entry, dark and yellow, spotted with straw mats of snowy whiteness; every thing bespoke comfort, neatness, and a farmer's rude wealth. The rooms were nearly all of the quaint pattern, large, high-ceiled, and heavily-corniced, with oaken framing, and but one was fitted up in modern style. This was the front room on the east side of the dwelling, and rejoiced in a carpet of rich pattern and coloring; a pianoforte, two or three couches, a beautiful desk of some West India wood, and chairs massive and polished. Here might often be seen little Jessie Goreham, the fair lily of the family, her soft, light hair braided about a brow of surpassing whiteness; her blue eyes wandering dreamily from object to object; her little fingers busily plying knitting-needles, or touching the notes of the piano, her father's birthday present. When she played after the day's work was done, Farmer Goreham might always be found outside of the parlor-door on the broad straw settee, handkerchief over his face, listening to every music-dropping note. Honest Ben stood six feet and four inches. He was a powerful, swarthy-browed, and handsome man; had been a hard, earnest worker, and as laborious a thinker. Authors of wondrous research stood upon the shelves in his library; books that were born of and for capacious and far-reaching intellect were his daily study. His wife was what would be called a gentle, ladylike woman, famous for her housekeeping qualities, and noticeable for her great reverence for her tall husband. They had but two children, Jessie and Herman, their pride, and their greatest earthly blessing.

It was a pleasant, red twilight, just after a refreshing shower. Mrs. Goreham was walking reflectively through rows of early pears, all put up in baskets as white as drifted snow.

"Sarah," she said, to a red-cheeked girl, "I know Mrs. Wise at the hotel would like some of these pears; suppose you pick out a hand-basket full, and carry them up in the morning."

"I'll do so," said the girl.

"And don't let any thing happen to the eggs again—you broke three this morning. Not that I care for the eggs, but your habits are somewhat careless, and I wish you to correct them."

"Yes 'm," said Sarah, demurely.

In the door-way, watching the great piles of drifted clouds, stood Jessie and her father. Both of them wore a touching sadness in cheek and eye. The mother, as she looked at them, grew sad also, even to tears, for she took out her handkerchief, and silently wiped her eyes.

"There he is," said Jessie, in a low, almost broken voice.

"And no letter, I fear, from our poor boy," said honest Ben as he watched the motions of the coming lad with eagle eyes.

The boy came nearer—handed a letter; the father took it, and shook his head as he sighed, " Not from Herman."

"And nearly five months," murmured the farmer's wife, gently.

"Yes, nearly five months since we began to wonder whether the poor boy were dead or alive. Well, Heaven give us strength."

"We thought so much of him," mused the fond mother.

"If we could hear aught—but this dreadful uncertainty," groaned the farmer

"Terrible! and in that place where they strangle men with the garotte, for no offense but that of loving liberty," sighed the wife, in response.

Jessie had crept into the parlor, and opened the lately-unused instrument. As she touched the familiar chords, her hands trembled, and the tears rolled down her pale cheeks.

"I can't bear to hear it," said the old farmer.

"Nay, father, let the child alone; it soothes her. She feels the loss as keenly as either of us," pleaded his wife. " Ask her to play for us; it will cheer her up, poor little thing; and he loved music—why should not we ? Play, Jessie, play, dear," she called, through the open door; "one of thy father's favorites, my child." So Jessie sat there, and, by the moonlight, played softly all her father's favorite harmonies.

The great corner-clock in the entry struck nine, when there was a hurried knock at the door. It was the post-boy again.

"I knew you were looking all the time for letters from away," he said; "and so, as this came in late, I made bold to bring it."

The farmer thanked him. His great, brown hands trembled as he took from the case his silver-rimmed spectacles, and fumbled over the letter long before his eyes rested upon it.

He dreaded to read the superscription. Alas! he was doomed again to disappointment. The hand was femininely delicate; it was post-marked New York. He threw it on the table, and turned away impatiently.

"Oh, rather, won't you read it? What beautiful writing!" cried Jessie.

"No, I don't want to read it. It's an order, likely, for fruit or butter—it's nothing that I want to see."

"Benjamin, Benjamin; thee must be more reconciled," said Mrs. Goreham, who, having been brought up a Friend, used the language of that sect whenever she felt strongly excited.

"May I read it, father?" asked Jessie.

"Yes, read it, child, read it."

Jessie opened the letter, but she had scarcely read the first dozen lines, when she uttered a great cry of joy.

"O mother! O father! it is of Herman, after all. So wonderful! still he's not found; but she—oh! stop, I'll read it, you'll be so astonished—perhaps so delighted—I don't know; it's very sad;" and thus, alternating from joy to pathos, she commenced what follows:

MRS. GOREHAM—*Dear Madam:* I felt toward you the emotions of a daughter when I first heard my Herman (pardon me, but in life or death he is still mine), speak of the virtues of his sweet mother. I should not take the liberty of addressing you thus, though probably my name is not new to you, were I not driven to the direst necessity. Your son took passage for himself and me in the bark Eagle, from Cuba; put me on board, and then returned for some important matters left behind, and I have not seen him, neither heard from him from that day to this. Where he is, how dealt with, God only knows! to that Great Being I have confided him, and await patiently the result. I am an orphan, far away from my family, who have conspired cruelly to unite me with a man for whom I have neither affection or even esteem, and I dare not return, for I am certain the wicked purpose that has been the aim of their lives would be put in execution. There are spies surrounding me, so that I am under the necessity of wearing a constant and disagreeable disguise, and even under that I fear I am recognized. I must tell you the whole of my miserable story I have begun. I have thrown myself on your kindness; I must not shrink, however pride may counsel me. I am compelled to add, that I have not now, and have not had, sufficient food to sustain life comfortably. I, who have all my life had delicacies at my command, am starving; my only food and drink has been a little dry bread and water. There, it is told; my trembling fingers have performed an unwilling task, but what could I do? If it were not for the hope I have of seeing him once more, I would give way to fainting nature, and die; but my faith forbids, and counsels me to take every needful precaution to sustain life. May I come to you, if only for a while? I should have been the happy wife of your son, if ill fate had not intervened. I can scarcely guide my pen for weakness and dizziness, and can only add, that, if on Thursday you will come, or send for me—for I have no means—you will find me at a grocer's on the corner of A——— and L——— streets.

Very truly yours,
MINERVA DE MONSERATE.

"The poor child!" cried the farmer's wife, tears in her eyes.

"Isn't it terrible, mamma?" murmured Jessie, her fair face troubled, and her large eyes distended; "it makes me shiver from head to foot to think of any one suffering, actually *suffering* for want of food, and only think of our abundance."

"Well, what would you do, mother?" asked the farmer, hastily.

"Do? take her home here, the poor child; take her right home. Do you go after her, father? she shall find rest here; think! she would have been the wife of our dear boy." Here the motherly heart gave way, her voice faltered and fell she arose, and hastily left the room.

"And Herman used to write such beautiful letters about her," said Jessie; "how I long to see her. He told me I should love her, and I know I shall. Father, is it not strange? What can we do to find Herman? We must go to Cuba, father; we must search from one end of the island to the other." Her beautiful eyes were bright and humid with tears.

3

" Yes, yes, child; but if they have put him out of the way—these Spaniards are devils when their blood is hot," he said, huskily ; " I wish he had staid at home, the poor boy."

———

While they were thus talking, Minerva sat in the dimness and solitude of her own room. Candle she had none, but the moon shone now and then with a brightness that penetrated even into the somber corner, and played about her poor, pale face, with its white lips, and burning eyes. Every day for nearly a month she had known that the prowling Spaniard walked to and fro before her door, as if fiendishly to intimate that go where she would, he should keep guard, and be in readiness to deliver her, if possible, into the hands of her uncle. This unmanly surveillance on the part of her persecutor had worn upon the poor girl, till she had become almost emaciated, and the want of proper food, added to her constant mental anguish, threatened to prostrate her with a long and dangerous illness.

Once the man had written to her—she had flung his letter in the fire. Scores of times he had attempted to see her, but she was resolute, and had never allowed him to enter her door. Weak and despairing, she had given up hope, and looked forward to death with longing. She had even, when the delirium of hunger was upon her, revolved in her mind the different modes of suicide, and once she had actually obtained some charcoal, and closed her doors and windows, in the expectation of putting an end to her unhappy existence. It is strange how often, by the merest chance, the contemplation of a crime becomes suddenly as horrible as it had before seemed plausible. The simple fact of an humble neighbor, sent at the night-time by an overruling Providence, with a basin of soup, with the modest assurance that she had thought the lady looked ill, and would relish it, changed the current of her destiny. The air of the room seemed fierce and hot; its darkness tomb-like, and Minerva, like one awaking from a trance, rushed to the windows, and, throwing them open, breathed once more (her tears gushing the while,) the delightful air, murmuring, " I was insane, Father, forgive me ! help me to bear the burden till thou shalt see fit to remove it." This little prayer gave her a relish for more. Strengthened and comforted by the nourishment, she still farther supplicated that the Almighty would deliver her from the power of her oppressors, and arose, feeling a certainty that in some way help was soon to come. That afternoon she overlooked her slender wardrobe. Noticing that there was some rattling substance in the pocket of an apron, she drew out an old letter, one she recognized immediately as having been written by Herman while he was at his home. "Saratoga"—the name she had tried so often and so vainly to remember. An impulse seized her, of which she determined to take instant advantage. She would write a letter to his home—to his mother, and throw herself upon their protection. The idea was as suddenly acted upon, the letter written, and sent as cautiously as she could manage it, and now she gave herself time to think. What the result would be, she did not dare imagine. Sometimes she was bewildered with hope; again, fearing that she might be deemed an impostor, her heart sank; but be as it might, she believed that in some way deliverance would come.

The third day, early in the morning, she dressed herself in her wonted habit, and, taking a few articles with her, set out on her promised errand. The man at whose shop she rested offered her a chair, remarking that she looked weary. He had seen her before, and doubtless thought her appearance as remarkable as it was unique, so singular was the blending of youth and age in her countenance—the gray hair, the large spectacles, the mimic furrows, and the bright young eyes and lips, full, though not blooming. Trembling, even shivering as one in an ague, she sat near the warm sunlight of an August day, waiting, dreading, hoping—above all, hoping! At the sound of wheels, how wistfully she looked forth! Now it was the baker's cart, now a market-wagon—oh! after all her longing desires, was she to be doomed to disappointment? Presently a light Jersey wagon, covered, drawn by a handsome gray horse, came by—drove more slowly—backed a little, and stopped. Poor Minerva! her eyes grew dim—she clutched at the counter convulsively. That face—the handsome, brown, kindly face, so like the son's. Oh! she could have shrieked for very joy. It must be for her.

"Is there a lady waiting here to go out of town?"

"Yes, yes," cried Minerva, eagerly; he turned, astonished, glancing at her narrowly, looked at the small, white hand, now ungloved, smiled as he gave another scrutinizing gaze at the oldish bonnet and the odd face, and clasped the little fingers in his, locking his lips together. His eyes shone suspiciously, his lips trembled as he said, "Are you all ready?"

"All ready," she replied, low and brokenly.

"Then come," he drew her arm in his, as tenderly as if he had been twenty-one, and she a bride, assisted her into the wagon, and drove off at a brisk pace. The hunted fawn was free, at least for the present.

———

CHAPTER XII.

TWO ARRIVALS.

TEN minutes had not elapsed, when a lumbering carryall, drawn by an impatient, high, black horse, drove als oup to the grocer's store. A man dressed in a farmer's suit of gray, with long hair, that dangled beneath his hat in glittering skeins, keen, dark eyes, encased by horn spectacles, and a hand singularly small and well gloved, sprang out and entered the store.

"Is there a lady waiting here to go in the country?" he inquired, hastily, after a quick scrutiny.

"You're too late, old gentleman," said the grocer, speaking very slowly, as he always did when he was busy; "she's gone with the t'other old man, maybe he was your brother."

"How long has she been gone?" queried the man, with short imperative words. His manner offended the grocer.

"Well, it may be half-an-hour, it might be five minutes; I don't keep the run of all the people who go out of my shop, the run of their custom is all I care about," he replied, slower than before.

"So much for the cursed breakage," muttered the man, as he walked to the door, and scanned first up and down the street. "If the rotten shaft had held good, just twenty minutes longer, she would have been in my possession, now it remains to head her off in that direction, and that will be difficult."

As he said this to himself, he had sprang into the vehicle, showing a row of teeth, glittering and white as milk, while his upper lip, shorn of a recent mustache, proved by its quivering jerks, the agitation of his mind, and the fierceness of his temper.

Meanwhile, the gray had cleared the lower part of the city, before the old farmer turned his attention from the prospect before him. Then, when they were past all danger, for the horse was spirited, and pricked up his ears at the sight of a bridge or railroad track, he said, pointing to the bottom of the carriage, "There's a little basket there, mother put me up a few sandwiches and cakes, for, to tell you the truth, I started without my breakfast. Perhaps you will help me eat them, it's not so pleasant to eat alone."

Minerva thanked him, blessing him in her heart for his thoughtfulness and delicacy, blessing him for the food, for she was hungry.

"I must look strange to you, in this disfiguring dress," she said, and as she spoke, she lifted the bonnet, cap, and false front from her head. Her own curls fell on the instant in thick masses about her face, that now, divested of spectacles, though white and thin, was still youthful, and very beautiful.

"Poor child!" said the old man, and there he paused. The past crowded on his soul, Herman, his face exultant with love and triumph, seemed at the moment, shadow-like, to sit beside his betrothed.

"You are ill," he added, a moment after, controlling his feelings; "how much you must have suffered! but we'll soon get you up again in our good country-air, clear and bracing, and my little Jessie longs to welcome you as a sister."

"Oh, yes, little Jessie," murmured Minerva; "he used to speak of her. How I shall love her!"

"I want to talk with you about my boy, when we get home," said the farmer; "I can't do it in the noise of these rattling wheels. But, perhaps, if you have found it necessary to wear your disguise, it is not prudent to take it off now, even though we are on the road to the country."

"It seems so pleasant to be free from the odious thing,"

said Minerva, childishly, "but I will replace it, and content myself with the beautiful fields, the clear sweet breeze, oh! how sweet!" She sank back in the carriage, and let her eyes rove delightfully round. Here, for the time, was peace and content. Herman's father had believed her, she was beside him, how strong and beautiful he seemed! and, oh! to be folded to his heart and called daughter—was that blissful time ever to be? should she who had been denied so long, know the blessings of a parental love? Quietly she sat there, too happy even to think, wanting to cry out with all her heart at the fresh beauty of the scarlet thorn-berry, and the clusters of ripening barberries, that made the road like a picture, at the yellow hay-stacks in the fields, flinging invisible censers of perfume, at the cottages and farm-yards, laughing to herself with an almost infantile glee, as she thought of Senor Velasquez, pacing back and forth, the self-constituted sentry over an empty room. Little she dreamed how near she had been to falling in his hateful power, but the space of fifteen minutes ago.

That morning was one of excitement and anxiety, at the pleasant farm-house. It had been impossible for honest Ben to eat the nice breakfast, so neatly prepared by his wife, and Jessie was fluttering from mother to father, restless almost to tears. She did cry a little, when her father set out, and said, with her last kiss, "Be *sure* and bring her, father."

Her mother seeing that she grew more nervous as the time wore on, planned that she should carry some little delicacy to the sick lady at the hotel, and put up for her some of her choicest fruit. Mrs. Wise had been an early friend of Mrs. Gorcham, and in her sad illness had wished to be near her. Jessie was an especial favorite with the sick woman, and she loved to see the bright, young face in her darkened chamber. Jessie was there perhaps an hour. She came home brimful of news.

"Mother, what do you think?" she exclaimed, her voice eager, her eyes shining; "who do you think has come to the hotel?"

"Some great personage, I should judge, by your manner, my daughter," was the quiet reply.

"Yes, a general with a long name, a Spanish general from

Cuba, and there's no telling how rich he is. They say such
quantities of baggage as he has brought, and so many servants! I saw a chariot myself, or rather, Mrs. Wise called it
a *volante*, open ; and the harness glittered with silver and gold,
and there was a negro sitting on one of the horses, I declare
I never saw such a splendid uniform—and—"

"Livery, my child," said Mrs. Goreham.

"Oh, yes! well it was as brilliant as it could be, and such
horses! I thought father's gray was the handsomest horse I
ever saw, but these are both milk-white, two beauties. Then
there's a sister, I haven't found out yet whether young or old,
and a very handsome Spanish gentleman, Mrs. Wise, says,
though she don't like his eyes."

"Well, and what does it all amount to?" asked the mother,
not at all dazzled by this enumeration.

"Why, nothing—that is," said Jessie, slowly, hesitating as
she wound the blue strings of her hat round and round her
finger; "of course they are people of distinction and wealth,
enormous wealth, Mrs. Wise says."

"But there are a great many people of wealth and distinction, here," said Mrs. Goreham.

"Yes, but nobody has made such a sensation, so Mrs. Wise
says; *everybody* is talking about it, and he has engaged almost
a whole floor, two parlors, three or four bedrooms, and two
or three rooms besides. They have their breakfast carried up
to them, for I suppose they feel themselves too good to eat
with the rest of the boarders. Mrs. Wise says, she heard that
they carried their priest with them, for they are all very pious.
Oh, dear! how I should like to see them!"

"Some one is coming, I shall like to see far better," said
Mrs. Goreham, rising and shaking out the folds of her dress;
her quick ear had detected the sound of coming wheels.

"Oh, patience, me! yes, I'd almost forgotten," said Jessie,
with flushed face; "I wonder who she will look like? I
wonder if I shall like her? Oh, dear!" and her little face
fell again; "these great people came from Cuba. I almost
hate the name, but, perhaps, why, who knows, but they may
help us, fiend Herman?"

Mrs. Goreham smiled sadly at the ludicrous idea. That
these grandees were in any way connected with the fate of

her boy, a plain farmer's son, never remotely occurred to her mind.

The wheels were nearer; even father's voice could be heard speaking to the boy who tended the gate. The mother fell back a little; Jessie grew very solemn as the carriage came in sight. At first only the portly form of the farmer was visible, and Jessie was ready to cry out with disappointment, but in another moment it was plainly to be seen that a woman occupied the seat behind.

Minerva had disengaged her uncomely disguise before she was handed out. The flash of expectation crimsoned her cheeks—her eyes were eager, large, and bright as diamonds.

"See what I've brought you home," said the old farmer. His wife received the stranger with open arms, kissed her fondly, pressed her hand with earnest love. Jessie put her arm around her, thinking to herself, "Oh! how beautiful! I'm sure I shall love her dearly!"

"Take her right up-stairs, Jessie, daughter," said her mother, gazing with yearning fondness on the gentle girl for her son's sake, and when she has rested both of you come down to breakfast.

It seemed like heaven to Minerva after her prison-like life, thus to be brought into genial sunshine, among simple, kindly hearts. She looked around the large chamber so scrupulously clean—everywhere only white, from bed hangings to the lilies resting in clear crystal on the mantel-piece. She looked out —there were no lawns, no fountains, no ornamental grounds, but the handiwork of the great God, grander than all the arts of men, was stamped upon crowned hills, and the blue and amber skies.

"This is rest," she said to Jessie, who was as fully occupied as she could be in gazing her fill at the lovely stranger, and wondering so heartily where Herman could be. And when they went down-stairs to the simple luxuries spread out before them—the fresh honey, the stamped butter, the white breakfast-cakes, Minerva thought she had never seen so much elegance. Meantime, the farmer and his wife, after consulting together about her, had determined that she must still be kept as secluded as possible, and that every means must be taken to restore the faded bloom to her cheek. That evening, the farmer held a long consultation with her. He did not dare to tell either her or his wife that he had just heard how a vessel had been wrecked off the coast of Cuba, at or near the time that Herman had intended to sail.

———

CHAPTER XIII

DORA'S PROPOSITION.

SENOR ABRATES walked the floor impatiently. His arms were folded and his brow seemed to deepen in frowns at every step. His petted sister reclined upon a couch as was her wont, idly toying with her fan.

"Come, Manuel, get a carriage and give me a drive," she said coaxingly, lifting herself a little from the mass of silken velvet.

"I'm not in the mood for a drive," was the reply.

"No—I expect as much. You never are in a mood for a drive or for any thing else. now-a-days. I never saw such a stupid thing as you have grown to be—perfectly mulish—no, or yes, to every thing, nothing more. For my part I wish Minerva Monserate had never put herself under your horse's heels. for you've not been the same man since."

"Be silent, Dora—you talk foolishly."

"I talk truth, and you know it. Fie, there are a dozen handsomer girls than she. I could point them out this minute. Carrie Bradley, why she's a perfect Juno, in comparison—Minerva had but a milk-and-water beauty; and there's Margaret Holmes, isn't she splendid? Either of them I fancy would compensate for the loss of——"

"Silence!" exclaimed her brother, angrily.

"I should like to know who you think you are talking to, sir?" said Dora, with such an assumption of dignity, as she arose from her seat and threw back her small head, that her brother could not forbear a laugh in the midst of his passion.

"To a foolish little child," he said good-naturedly, "who

does not know what she is talking about, who can not quite read the thoughts even of her own brother."

"So foolish, too, that she can't be trusted with any of her brother's troubles," said Dora with some pique.

"Why should I burden you?"

"You needn't; tell me what your trouble is, and I'll laugh it out of you," she answered.

"The troubles of a grown man are not so easily laughed off, my wise little sister," was the reply.

"Well, at venture, I'm certain it's about that Monserate," she said.

"It's about two or three Monserates," was his rejoinder.

Dora sat bolt upright now. "Why! are they going to give you any trouble because she was here?"

"Not unless that sneaking Velasquez meddles—but he will."

"Oh, yes; he owes you a grudge."

"He owes me a dozen."

"Well, what can he do?"

"That's just what I don't know.

"But we needn't return to Cuba this year, at least, if **we** don't wish; they could hardly trouble us."

"But they are here."

"What, the great general here, in New York?"

"No—the little general with the great name, not in New York city, but in Saratoga."

"Oh! at Saratoga! I wonder if he will marry any one from there?"

"A woman—a woman!" cried Senor Abrates, snapping his fingers.

"Pshaw!" ejaculated Dora, with a look of great contempt —"that's your cry, always. But I see—Velasquez will tell them you loved her and have secreted her; it might make trouble, especially as we have whole trunks full of her clothes."

"And he will, if I can find no way to prevent it."

"Manuel," asked Dora, after a thoughtful pause, "where do you suppose she is?"

"If I knew," was the gloomy reply, "you would not need to ask me that question."

"I have sometimes thought that perhaps she grew tired of life," mused Dora.

"No, there were no indications of such a thing," replied Manuel; "she loved that fellow who deserted her too well," he added with unusual bitterness.

"And Manuel, I have just thought," said little Dora, with an air of importance and a very solemn face; "how can we tell but Senor Velasquez has spirited her off and perhaps married her himself."

Manuel paused suddenly in his walk, struck by her words.

"I never thought of it, and he is so finished a villain, too. I wish I was certain of her fate," he continued, traversing the floor again. "At any rate, my conscience is clear. I have tried every method I know of in vain; she has baffled me," he sighed heavily.

"I'll tell you what to do, Manuel."

"Well, what?"

"Go to Saratoga."

"Yes, to show you off," he half laughed, half sneered.

"I have a fancy to see the general, and oh! if that magnificent Don Carlos *has* come, about whom I have heard so much—what would I not give to have a look at him? But that is not all," she hurried to say—"the step will disarm them of suspicion—they certainly could not believe that you would leave such a woman in New York, alone."

"There is something in that," said her brother.

"Then again, it may be that Miss Minerva stole quietly to Cuba, repenting of her misdeeds, and for reward, they have brought her to Saratoga."

"Your imagination is fertile," was his reply.

"Still, you can not say that it might not be. Women have changed their minds from time immemorial. I should like to see her. I never met with any one who interested me so much on some accounts. If I were you, I'd meet this rich Cuban more than half way, or else he may demand an explanation, and with your peculiar sentiments, that may make you appear rather foolishly."

Manuel looked at his sister in astonishment. He had never known her to be so voluble on any subject but dress, and now her arguments seemed to carry a weight with them that was

by no means to be despised. He did not know that gratifica-
tion of self was her main object, and that nothing is more
likely to call for eloquence than a plea for our own wants, a
recital of one's own wrongs or pleasures.

"It strikes me that we will go to Saratoga," said Manuel
after some moments of thought. His heart leaped at the bare
supposition of meeting Minerva Monserate. He loved her
with a true and fervent passion that threatened to be as last-
ing as it was sincere.

Dora exulted inwardly. To see Saratoga, was the climax
of her traveling ambition. She had heard exaggerated accounts of its fashions, its resorts, its occupants, and her vain
little heart fluttered at the possibility of the sensation and the
conquests she might make. Visions of rich dresses stretched
out before her imagination; she was as ambitious as Senora
Mancha herself. It was settled that in three days at the least
they would start for the far-famed watering-place. Meantime,
Manuel engaged rooms.

CHAPTER XIV

THE CUBAN LION AT SARATOGA.

A picture of indolence and high-life almost unequaled. A long, private parlor, gorgeous with upholstery, some of which is imported expressly for the use of the occupant. The high windows, rich with hangings of gold-embroidered lace. A lounge of crimson velvet, drawn up to the central casement, and reclining thereon in voluptuous elegance, Don Carlos. Nothing could be more splendid than the oriental magnificence of his costume; it is an emulation of princely expenditure. It flashes if he lifts an arm as if embroidered with gems. The light trembles from shoulder to hem if he but moves. An amber pipe, gold-mouthed, and falling in many serpentine folds, is gracefully suspended from his lips. His smoking cap is of massive gold braid, with perhaps here and there a jewel touching its points. He is the king of loungers, this Don Carlos, with unbounded wealth—this heir to luxury.

He has been out to-day, but no languid and well-dressed belle was honored by a seat at his side in the beautiful volante. It has not yet come to that. The Don uses his gold, brilliant-mounted eye-glass, now and then, drawls " rather pretty," and that is all. His selfish heart is steeled against bright eyes—the charmer's charm in vain. He is watched through closed shutters—watched stealthily through half-open doors. The young fledglings go into extasies over him—his walk, his air, his bow, his smile, all are perfection. Decidedly he is the lion of Saratoga. And then there is such a romantic story going the rounds, how he is breaking his heart for some fair lady who ran away on the night she was to be a bride—poor man! no wonder he shuns the sex and keeps so much in solitude. And that dear little elderly lady! did you notice her laces? Every day something new and the plainest far more costly than the richest specimens that adorn the arms and bosoms of the fair Americans. What yellow glances some of those women bestow upon them—deeper than even the chronic jaundice-tinge of the wonderful webs. As for dresses, the ladies might search their wardrobes in vain to find any thing that will approach their marvelousness. She is an object of envy in spite of her diminutive face, and prospective wrinkles. Even the gold-mounted fan is a talisman in her hand. Who could hope to approach that subtle maneuvering that makes every motion a word? And so that is the aunt of the magnificent don, they say, and her diamonds fairly blind one.

Don Carlos still smokes and lounges. On an in aid table near are the evening papers, which, by their rumpled appearance, he has probably consulted. By-and-by he needs something, and calls his valet, who is in an outer room, to pull the bell-rope. Marques is a small, yellow man, very handsomely dressed. He walks with dignity up to the cord, gives it a delicate touch, and retires gracefully. One of the servants of the house appears.

"Call my waiter," says the don, with an air.

Presently the waiter, a thoroughly black negro, dressed in white, enters, bowing obsequiously. Don Carlos points to the little gilt basin in which his pipe rests; it needs replenishing. The waiter, with another servile inclination, performs his master's bidding. This only to give an insight into the private habits of the Cuban lion.

A little later General Monscrate entered, precisely dressed and perfumed.

"Well, guardy," said the young man, turning himself a little as the general threw his delicate frame upon another lounge; "what have you been doing to-day?"

"Scarcely any thing of importance," was the reply; "I am waiting to gather up my forces—we are making an impression now."

"Are we?" queried the don, languidly, casting his eye along his dressing-gown; "well, that is what we came for, you know."

"I don't see as we get any nearer to the matter in hand. This story Velasquez repeats in his last letter, leaves us where we were before."

" You mean that Abrates has concealed her ?"

" Yes."

" Married her, perhaps," said the don, in an undertone, his face growing gray.

" Perhaps."

"If he has!" murmured the young man, between his teeth.

" What can you do ?"

" At least, kill him," shouted the don, with ferocity.

A servant came in and handed the general a note, then disappeared.

" Aha !" cried the general, as he read; " this brings news. Senor Velasquez is below-stairs."

Don Carlos started bolt upright.

" Let him come up immediately," he said, taking an easier attitude.

It was not long before the door opened, and a tall man, in the dress of a clergyman, entered. He was smoothly shaven, wore his hair low upon the forehead, and spectacles of a greenish color disguised his eyes. Both the general and the don expressed by their glances the utmost astonishment.

" We had looked for a friend," said the general, frowning at this intrusion as he considered it.

" And not for an interloper," added the don, haughtily.

The incomer was silent, but with one movement his shining black hair was thrown back, and the spectacles displaced.

" Senor Velasquez !" cried the general.

" Hollo ! old friend," ejaculated the don, laughing heartily. " Where in the world did you study theology ?"

" My theology all came out of your books," said the senor, smiling, as he seated himself. " So you did not know me; I was certain you would not. I flatter myself that few can carry out a disguise better than myself. Well, I'm glad to see you. So you thought best to follow my advice, and come here in person ?"

" We followed the dictates of our own judgment," said the don, more coolly. " I intended to come from the first; a slight indisposition prevented me, however."

A lurking smile grew deeper on the thin lips of Senor V₁
lasquez.

"Well, what's the business?" asked the don, laying hi
costly pipe aside. "What have you found out—what do yo:
know?"

"I have by letter given you a precise account of my do
ings up to the present time," said the senor. "I have now
only to exonerate Senor Abrates; she escaped him, as well
as myself."

"How do you know?" inquired the don.

"I have seen her," was the reply.

"Where? when?" cried Don Carlos, excitedly.

"Patience, my dear friend," said the senor, softly; "I will
tell you the whole story. For some reasons, probably of im·
portance, Senorita Monserate left the house of Senor Abrates.
I tracked her to a common boarding-house, where she had
taken rooms under the name of Smith. For some time I
watched her, waiting for an opportunity to surprise her; but
before that could happen, she had changed her name again,
and her lodgings. For weeks I tried in vain to obtain an interview with her. I have waited patiently before the house
in which she was, for hours at a time. I have tracked her to
stores and the post-office, but she was too cunning for me. I
have every reason to suspect that she knew me. One day I
saw a boy go from the house with a letter. I knew then that
she would not venture out. I followed the boy and overtook
him. I wished to see the letter—he was not to be threatened.
I bribed him; he carefully unsealed it, for the seal was yet
wet, and, for a half-sovereign, allowed me to read it. It was
a plan for flight. On a certain day she was to meet the man
to whom she had written, and place herself under his protection. Thus forewarned, I thought I might outwit her. I obtained a country suit and wagon, and should assuredly have
been successful, but for the breaking of my shafts in going
down-hill. The accident delayed me nearly half an hour, and
I was in the vicinity of no other carriage. When I arrived
there, she had gone. If I had found her—" he paused here,
but "*you* would never have seen her," gleamed in his crafty
eye.

"Too bad!" muttered the don, making as if he would

walk; then changing his mind, throwing himself down again, where he crouched with folded arms, deep in thought.

"Had you no clue in the letter by which you might trace her?" asked the don, excitedly.

"I certainly had," was the reply.

"Well, well; where was it?"

"I have gone beyond the bounds of my contract already," replied Senor Velasquez, evasively.

"Five hundred dollars for the information," said Don Carlos; adding, with a sneer, "you make money on me."

"That's the way I live," was the reply.

"I'll give you a check, now, for the information.'

"Well, then, she is at this moment not a hundred miles from this hotel," was the crafty reply.

"I thought so!" exclaimed Don Carlos, springing up. "But where—where?"

"That I must first find out myself," replied Senor Velasquez. "The greatest caution is necessary, now, for she is with powerful friends. In this disguise, however, I hope to succeed. You have, of course, taken the precaution of entering another name on the books?"

"Yes," replied Don Carlos; "the general assumes the name Ameyda, and I that of Don Johan—ha! ha! My venerable aunt, who had the liberty of choosing her own *sobriquet*, is Dona Marguerita—quite fanciful. Our servants are drilled, so there's no fear, unless the lady sees our precious faces."

"That is all well; in my ministerial character, I flatter myself I can succeed in reaching her presence. This much I have learned, that she is in a large farm that is very favorably situated for the purpose of abduction; for it must, I fear, come to force at last. Leave me alone to manage by what artifice I can best serve your purpose. In the mean time, we are to have two more of our friends here, Senor and Senorita Abrates."

"How do you know that?" inquired the don.

"Their names are booked. I don't doubt but that they will be here to-day."

"I remember the little senorita," mused Don Carlos; "she was a pretty little thing, and quite took my fancy. Of dif-

A lurking smile grew deeper on the thin lips of Senor Velasquez.

"Well, what's the business?" asked the don, laying his costly pipe aside. "What have you found out—what do you know?"

"I have by letter given you a precise account of my doings up to the present time," said the senor. "I have now only to exonerate Senor Abrates; she escaped him, as well as myself."

"How do you know?" inquired the don.

"I have seen her," was the reply.

"Where? when?" cried Don Carlos, excitedly.

"Patience, my dear friend," said the senor, softly; "I will tell you the whole story. For some reasons, probably of importance, Senorita Monserate left the house of Senor Abrates. I tracked her to a common boarding-house, where she had taken rooms under the name of Smith. For some time I watched her, waiting for an opportunity to surprise her; but before that could happen, she had changed her name again, and her lodgings. For weeks I tried in vain to obtain an interview with her. I have waited patiently before the house in which she was, for hours at a time. I have tracked her to stores and the post-office, but she was too cunning for me. I have every reason to suspect that she knew me. One day I saw a boy go from the house with a letter. I knew then that she would not venture out. I followed the boy and overtook him. I wished to see the letter—he was not to be threatened. I bribed him; he carefully unsealed it, for the seal was yet wet, and, for a half-sovereign, allowed me to read it. It was a plan for flight. On a certain day she was to meet the man to whom she had written, and place herself under his protection. Thus forewarned, I thought I might outwit her. I obtained a country suit and wagon, and should assuredly have been successful, but for the breaking of my shafts in going down-hill. The accident delayed me nearly half an hour, and I was in the vicinity of no other carriage. When I arrived there, she had gone. If I had found her—" he paused here, but "*you* would never have seen her," gleamed in his crafty eye.

"Too bad!" muttered the don, making as if he would

walk; then changing his mind, throwing himself down again, where he crouched with folded arms, deep in thought.

"Had you no clue in the letter by which you might trace her?" asked the don, excitedly.

"I certainly had," was the reply.

"Well, well; where was it?"

"I have gone beyond the bounds of my contract already," replied Senor Velasquez, evasively.

"Five hundred dollars for the information," said Don Carlos; adding, with a sneer, "you make money on me."

"That's the way I live," was the reply.

"I'll give you a check, now, for the information.'

"Well, then, she is at this moment not a hundred miles from this hotel," was the crafty reply.

"I thought so!" exclaimed Don Carlos, springing up. "But where—where?"

"That I must first find out myself," replied Senor Velasquez. "The greatest caution is necessary, now, for she is with powerful friends. In this disguise, however, I hope to succeed. You have, of course, taken the precaution of entering another name on the books?"

"Yes," replied Don Carlos; "the general assumes the name Ameyda, and I that of Don Johan—ha! ha! My venerable aunt, who had the liberty of choosing her own *sobriquet*, is Dona Marguerita—quite fanciful. Our servants are drilled, so there's no fear, unless the lady sees our precious faces."

"That is all well; in my ministerial character, I flatter myself I can succeed in reaching her presence. This much I have learned, that she is in a large farm that is very favorably situated for the purpose of abduction; for it must, I fear, come to force at last. Leave me alone to manage by what artifice I can best serve your purpose. In the mean time, we are to have two more of our friends here, Senor and Senorita Abrates."

"How do you know that?" inquired the don.

"Their names are booked. I don't doubt but that they will be here to-day."

"I remember the little senorita," mused Don Carlos; "she was a pretty little thing, and quite took my fancy. Of different stuff from Senorita Minerva, she would allow caresses; while my little playmate (a shadow crossed his forehead), what a life she led me! But I will show her yet whose turn it is to be master."

———

CHAPTER XV

THE VISIT TO WASHINGTON.

MINERVA was now comparatively at peace. Honest Ben was preparing for a journey to Washington. He had always promised Jessie that if ever he visited the capital of the nation, she should accompany him. A brother of the old farmer held a seat in the national legislature, and he had often expressed a hope that the old man might come on, and bring Jessie, to get acquainted with her cousins, whom she had never yet seen. Jessie was all in a glow of hope when she heard her father's proposal, but dared not appear too anxious, lest it might not seem quite courteous to their new friend; but when her father said, " Well, Jessie, what do you think about going with me ?" she exclaimed, " Oh! I should like it above all things."

" But it will not be quite polite to leave Miss Monserate alone in this old farm-house."

" Don't regard me a moment," said Minerva ; " I beg you will not. I should feel quite unhappy if Jessie staid at home for me. Go with your father, my dear Jessie, and God prosper his mission."

" I'll raise heaven and earth but what I find something about my boy," exclaimed the old man, fervently.

His wife's eye glistened with a tear as he said this, though at the same time she gently rebuked his vehemence.

" Well, Jessie," she said, stooping over her fondly, " father goes this day week ; so get ready."

Never bird flew more cheerfully about its nest, than Jessie around the house, gathering up her little finery. There were purchases to be made ; a hundred dollars were put in Jessie's little hands, at which she looked in unfeigned astonishment.

"I shall not want half of this," she said; "only think—one hundred dollars! it seems so much to spend at one time."

Minerva laughed quietly. "I used to give more than that for one dress alone," she said; "but as I look at it now, after having wanted for a dollar, it does not seem right to spend money that way."

"More than that for *one* dress!" exclaimed Jessie; "why, pray, how much did that cost?"

"Oh! it cost three hundred and fifty dollars for the material alone. It was what they call a kincob, of East Indian manufacture; thick silk, worked all over with gold thread. But my uncle paid for all these things. I remember his getting me a muslin once, so very fine that it looked like a web, and, in fact, when wet, could not be seen at all. It was very expensive and beautiful."

"Why! how wealthy your uncle must have been!" exclaimed Jessie, whose hundred dollars seemed now quite insignificant.

"Yes," Minerva replied in her quiet way; "he was, I expect, immensely rich."

"And so is this old Cuban general at the hotel." Jessie turned quite pale. She had been forbidden to mention the arrival in the presence of Minerva.

The latter looked up, a startled query in her eyes. Seeing the confusion in Jessie's face, her white lips trembled out the question—"For heaven's sake, what do you mean, my friend? A Cuban general in Saratoga? Then it must be my uncle. He has found that I am here. Oh, where shall I go now?"

At that moment the farmer's wife entered. Seeing Minerva unwontedly agitated, she inquired the reason, and was quite displeased with her daughter's thoughtlessness.

"Was your uncle's name the same as your own?" she asked Minerva.

"Yes, Monserate—General Limenes de Monserate," said the trembling girl.

"Then make yourself easy, for that is not the name. This

is General Ameyda, and the young man with him is Don
Johan.   Father went to the hotel, last night, so do not trouble
yourself.   Besides, if it had been your uncle, he would in all
probability have rented a cottage, and kept himself in strict
privacy, no, I do not think it is."

Somewhat reassured, Minerva voluntered to aid Jessie in
her needlework, for the time was short, and there was much
to do; but throughout the day, at intervals, the sickening
thought would recur, that perhaps she was within the reach
of her enemies, and she shuddered at the sound of carriage-
wheels, however distant, or at the tread of a footstep, and on
no account could she be left a moment alone.   The impression had more than once crossed her mind that these new-
comers were really her uncle and the don under assumed
names, and she felt at times an almost irrepressible desire to
see for herself, to know and be prepared for the worst.   The
days went on as usual, however, Minerva allowed herself but
limited recreation, and was then always accompanied by the
farmer and his daughter, besides Bruno, a splendid Newfound-
land dog, to whom the lonely girl had become strongly attached, and who seemed to reciprocate her affection.   The
farmer had made arrangements with his head-gardener to remove to the house with his wife while he should be gone, and
gave him strict charge respecting the young Cuban girl.

It was the sabbath, the next day the farmer was to start
for Washington, and all things were in readiness.   The trunks
strapped and locked, were in the hall.   Jessie's neat gray
traveling suit, with its little linen collar and sleeve-bands, lay
in the spare-chamber on the bed, all ready for her to tuck herself into.   Jessie was looking very grave as she entered the
carriage to go to church; it made her think of that prospective journey so near at hand, but when she came home, she
was marvelously talkative.   There was a minister in the pul-
pit, she said, a handsome-looking man, only he wore such
odious green spectacles, and after church, he spoke to her
father, and asked him if he had not a son, a young man, of
perhaps twenty-four or five.   "You may imagine how father
felt," added Jessie, volubly; "he answered, 'Yes,' and looked
so sad! just ready to cry.   The minister then went on to say,
that he knew father by his great likeness, and that he had

cause to remember Herman, for he saved his life when they
were together in a steamer, cruising among the West India
Islands. You know Herman has been everywhere," she added, turning to Minerva, who listened with breathless interest.
"Well, he went on to say, that he had a terrible attack of
cholera, which was then raging in several of the islands, and
that Herman stood over him a whole night and a part of the
next day, and it was owing to his unremitting exertions that
he was now alive. You can't think how father grasped him
by the hand, and I do believe he couldn't speak for wanting
to cry. Then he told about Herman, and the man clenched
his teeth together, and declared that he would suffer any thing
for that young man, that noble, self-sacrificing young man, he
called him. He asked what he could do, and told father to
command him in any way. Father asked him to dinner, but
he said Mr. Calderon, 'our minister,'" she added, turning to
Minerva, "had invited him to-day, but he would call on you.
mother, this week, he has ever so many little anecdotes to tell
about that 'noble young man.'"

"I shall be very glad to see him," said her mother, gently;
"or any one that can give me any news of my dear boy."

The day passed pleasantly, and the half-joyful, half-dreaded
Monday had come. Jessie's little heart was so full, that her
leave-taking was quite mournful, while even the good farmer's
"take care of yourself," as he touched the lips of his wife, and
pressed the hand of his guest, was almost inaudible.

Thus the farmer's wife and Minerva were quite alone till
noon. Then came the gardener, a stout, burly man, with a
wife as stout, but looking better natured than himself, both
able from all appearances to protect a houseful from any felo-
nious attack, she with tongue, and he with muscle. Minerva
continued to ramble cautiously, accompanied always by Mrs.
Gorcham, and the dog Bruno. One evening, when they came
home, just at dusk, they found a stranger in the parlor, who
gave his name as the Rev. Mr. Secales, and whom Mrs. Goreham recognized instantly by Jessie's description. Minerva, as
was usual with her when any one came, took her seat in a
recess and showed a very visible disinclination to be noticed,
or even to speak. She had caught a glimpse of a dark face,
the eyes covered by spectacles, but the impression, slight as it

was, was not favorable. She knew to-night, however, that he was talking of Herman, and strained her attention to the utmost that she might listen. But the tones of his voice, so soft, so silken, so monotonous, struck unpleasantly the vibrative chord in her heart. She did not ask herself why; indeed, she was scarcely conscious of the feeling, so occupied was her mind with various matters.

"It is getting quite dark, I will order lamps," said Mrs. Goreham.

"Oh, if it makes no difference to you, madam, it charms me to sit in this soft, meditative twilight. I dislike the garish lamp, and you may see, perhaps," he touched the spectacles, lightly, "that I have a sufficient reason. Five years ago, I was sun-struck, and in consequence, I suffer much with my eyes, indeed my sight is quite indifferent," he added, pathetically; "I fear that in time I may lose it altogether."

The words and the voice drew much upon the sympathies of the two listeners.

"I presume you have many fine walks around here," he said, a moment after.

"Very many," Mrs. Goreham, replied; "we of the house, however, confine ourselves to the farm. We have several pretty copses, and Mr. Goreham has laid out private roads that are well shaded, so that we never have need to use the public highway, except for the carriage."

"How large, may I inquire, is your farm, Mrs. Goreham?" asked the stranger. "I am making a few statistics, as I go along, for my own private journal."

"This west part of it, thrown into fields, woodland, and grazing ground, comprises some two hundred acres, the southerly part, under cultivation, is about forty acres, I think," replied Mrs. Goreham, unsuspiciously. "Mr. Goreham has arranged a very pretty park, that opens from the public promenade, which he used to throw open for visitors to the place, but they did so much damage to his choice trees, that he closed it up a year ago, and only now and then, on application, allows a few persons, of whose principles he is sure, to enter."

Minerva had risen and left the room.

"That young woman is your daughter, I presume," said

the stranger, looking after her. " Still, I do not see the resemblance to your son—"

" Oh, no ! my daughter and my husband are both in Washington," said Mrs. Goreham, quickly ; " this young lady is a friend of Jessie's."

" Your husband has gone on business connected with your son's disappearance, I believe ? will he remain long ?"

" Not more than two or three weeks," was the reply " Alas! I have almost given up all hope of my son's safety. Several circumstances have occurred to make us apprehensive that there has been foul play somewhere."

" It is very sad, very sad," said the clergyman ; applying a snowy handkerchief to the rim visible around his spectacles.

" He was a most noble specimen of manhood. Thanks to him that I am alive. I am really grateful to add also, though I hope you will not think it egotism in me, that I was so fortunate as to save him from the wrath of a Danish governor, once, who, for the breach of some trivial etiquette, which he thought Mr. Goreham had intentionally committed, threatened him with prison, and I know not what other extremes. Very fortunately, I belonged to the same secret order with him, and by my making it known, added to other interference, your son was set at liberty."

" I thank you," said Mrs. Goreham, holding out her hand. " Any courtesy shown to my son, I consider as shown to me."

The man arose to go. Just then, the moon nearly at its full, threw its soft light across the room, enveloping the stately figure of the stranger, with a misty, tremulous light.

" I trust, madam, I am not asking too much, when I say it would gratify me exceedingly to walk over your grounds, at my liberty. Pray do not consider me bold, but I have heard much of their beauty."

" With the utmost pleasure," said Mrs. Goreham, whose heart was overflowing toward the reverend friend of her son ; " You shall have our own private key." She drew a bunch from her pocket, and slipping off the largest, handed it to him. At that very instant, as he grasped it, somewhat overeagerly, in his long, white fingers, it occurred to her that she might be doing a very imprudent thing. But there was no danger, at least, from this saintly personage, and, as for Minerva, she should know nothing about it.

The stranger moved away in the moonlight. Once he turned, showing his glittering teeth as he laughed, muttering, "'Two weeks! I must make hay while the sun shines; I must be on the watch, night and day; and I will. Now for the hotel."

CHAPTER XVI.

THE BELLE OF SARATOGA.

SENORITA DORA was the belle of the Saratoga company. At her very first appearance, the reigning beauties paled and grew envious. So innocent her face, and yet so capable of passion, those dark, southern eyes   Besides, she was the most graceful creature that ever practiced attitudes, till they became a part of her very being. As with all Spanish women, her fan was the ruling charm. Donna Mancha used hers delightfully, but Dora ravishingly. To mark the wrist, white and delicate as a snow-flake, bend about the glittering stem, now poised with gleeful motion, now raised in gentlest abandonment, now falling so helplessly! It was a study to see her use it for the purpose of coquetry, very charming, better than smiles, false lips, and honeyed words.

Dora had been domiciled a week, and at once had conquered what all the rest had sighed for in vain, the attention of the great Cuban don. He confessed to himself, that she had grown marvellously handsome since he saw her last, it would be no harm, surely, to flirt with her a little.

Dora sat in her chamber, examining with mute attention a bouquet of lovely flowers. Her brother entered, flushed and hurried.

"Ah, Don Carlos sent you those."

"Don Johan," she said, roguishly.

"I forget, though he gave me a stabbing glance yesterday when I carelessly called him by his lawful name. Well Dora, it seems to me you are progressing."

"How?" Dora held a blushing face down close to the flowers.

"How! why do you ask? Can't I see? can't everybody see? Does he look, at, speak to, in any way notice the rest of the throng? I tell you, you have won him, if you are careful."

"Oh, no," said Dora, thoughtfully. "You remember what he has come for; he will never relinquish her. Would you?"

"Never; but he will. It is not love alone, but spite as well, that urges him on. I can see that he will ultimately try to win my pretty little sister. What a match! the richest fellow in all Havana."

"Oh, nonsense, Manuel;" but, nevertheless, a triumph-glance gave new luster to her eyes. "Ah! I see," she added, quickly; "you want the coast clear, you are thinking of our runaway guest. Selfish brother, mine!"

It was his turn to blush, and the red blood showed through the dark cheek.

"Dora," he said, half whispering; "I have heard that she is here."

"Actually, here! in this house," cried the girl, springing up gleefully.

"No, no, not so fast, but she is in Saratoga; and I wonder if you could not help me find her out?"

"If I find her, it will be for Don Carlos, of course," she whispered.

"Then I shan't trust you—I will try myself. By the way, you have a partner provided for to-night, I see," he added, as he noticed a gilt-edged billet upon the table. "That is good, for I wish to be away reconnoitering. I hope you will enjoy yourself," he said, going to the door.

"And I wish you all manner of success," was the playful rejoinder.

Dora then called for her maid, and an hour was idled away choosing dresses for the night.

"I wish I dared wear one of Senora Minerva's splendid dresses," said Dora; "there is nothing like them here."

"And why not, pray?" asked Coco, flippantly; "her trunks are here."

"*He* might know—or that little-eyed senorita."

"Pshaw! men never remember. Besides, it will look differently upon you, and you can change the trimmings. Do
wear the blue and gold; you will look like a queen."

"I wish I dared," murmured the vain girl.

Meantime, Coco had opened the trunk, and there it lay with
its superb laces—the beautiful thing by which Minerva had set
so slight value.

"Oh! I shall look so well! Take it out and try it on,
Coco. When one does change from simplicity, one might as
well change for splendor. There!" she added, as she sur-
veyed herself in the glass, "it fits as if it were made for me.
I will run the risk—I will wear it."

A murmur of delight greeted the entrance of the young
Spanish girl, as she came in, leaning on the arm of the magnificent Cuban. The general's brow darkened. Dona Mancha felt in her old heart the revival of the jealousy of her
youth and beauty. Under many a smile a dagger of envy
was concealed, ready to destroy.

"It seems to me he takes a great fancy to yon maid,"
whispered the withered senora to her brother, the general.

"Oh! no;" replied the latter, not betraying the uneasiness
he felt, "she is a countrywoman. One always feels differently towards them."

"Yes, I should judge so by his manner. He will take no
other lady out to-night. Really, they are a handsome couple,
and how richly she is dressed! Where have I seen a brocade
like that?—oh! yes, Minerva's kincob—that must be a kincob
—only I remember Minerva had light blue trimmings, and
those are dark blue."

The general had not listened to this dissertation—he was
all eyes, watching his ward narrowly, and when at the close
of the dance he saw him lead the pretty creature out on the
veranda, his lips grew peevish.

"It must not be, it shall not be," he muttered; "it would
ruin me."

Meanwhile the Don promenaded up and down the sheltered
gallery, Dora hanging on his arm, tossing her fan up in a be-
witching way, and catching it again, while the moonbeams,
quivering all over her, made the gems like white flame upon
her throat and arms.

"So you'll not return to school again," said the Don lightly.

"Oh, no, indeed. After I have seen all I can of this merry company, I shall go back to dear Cuba."

"And whose heart will you leave aching here? This young and passionate America does not stint in its admiration of beauty," he said, softly.

"Whose heart? Oh! as the girls used to say at Madame Zeigler's, 'I care for nobody, nobody cares for me.'"

"Can you say that with truth?" asked the Don, bending more closely to her.

"With as much truth as such questions merit," she answered, unconscious of the rebuke implied.

"Oh! I beg your pardon," he said, haughtily.

"Indeed, you have no need to," she replied, with schoolgirl archness. "And I will tell you truly, that I have left no aching heart here—that I know of."

"Ah! some arrows wound at random," said the Don, growing more and more sentimental; "and are none the less fatal because they are shot carelessly."

"You are poetical," said Dora, mischievously.

"How can I help it! The moonlight, the music, and you," he said, expressively. "Before you came I was not inspired."

"Oh! Don Johan," she cried, reprovingly, then hesitated.

"Well!" he said, impatiently.

"How can I help listening to the romantic story that is going the rounds. Every lady tells it in detail, and I happen to know more than all the rest."

A short emphatic "well," followed.

"Why, the story goes that you are looking for a lost love," she said, with admirable simplicity. "But I need not speak of what others say. I have both seen and known her. Indeed, I think her very beautiful, Senor Johan."

The Don was silent a moment. I don't know but in spite of his admiration, he could have shaken her a little for this untimely piece of gossip.

"You speak of Senora Monserate," he said, quietly.

"Yes, she was very lovely."

"You thought so?"

"Of course I did; and you know so."

"I have seen lovelier," he said, thoughtfully. The little

minx beside him trembled. She only wanted to be sure that he did not love this rival—then !

"Yes ; I fancied once she was perfection," he added, in a low, smothered voice; "but I have changed my mind. Señorita, if she were here to-night, and you were by, I would dance with none but you."

"Oh ! senor, do not talk in this way to me," said the vain little creature, her voice tremulous, but with exultation.

"If you say it is displeasing to you, senorita, I will not."

She was only silent.

"Then, since you do not forbid me, I will add that it would have made me very unhappy if you had."

"If I had answered you ?"

"If you had *forbidden* me—yes, I should have been unhappy."

"The night air is chilly," whispered Dora

"But you *did not !*" emphatically said the Don. As they entered tthe hall, they almost stumbled over the little figure of the general. Had he been listening ? Perhaps not; he was surely going toward the assembly-room.

"Ah ! guardy—were you looking after me ?" asked the Don, suspiciously.

"I was about to find you," answered the general in a surly voice; "somebody is waiting for you."

"Ah ! and who is that somebody ? Let me lead the señorita to a seat, and I will join you again."

When the Don came out, the general stood moodily in the doorway.

"Well, who is it ?" queried the Don in his old, curt way.

"Velasquez."

"Ah ! couldn't he thrust his clerical visage upon us some other night, as well ? Where is he ?"

"In my room ; I had him shown there. And look here, Carlos, don't trust too much to that man."

"What ! *you* grown suspicious ?" laughed his ward.

"Yes, I confess I think the man a rascal. I deemed it best just to say to you, don't leave too much in his hands."

"Oh ! thank you—well—"

"And Carlos—"

"Johan," whispered the Don.

"Johan—then—you—I—confess I don't like your intimacy with that portionless senorita; and, I beg your pardon," he said, humbly, seeing the flashing eyes of the Cuban; "but they talk of it."

"They, who?"

"Everybody. They say she has thoroughly infatuated you."

An imprecation burst from the lips of the Don.

"You know where my hopes are placed," said the general, pathetically. "I do not think you would wrong one who has done so much for your interests."

"Pshaw!" said the young man, impatiently; "can I look at no one else? Must I taboo my eyesight?"

"No, no; I was only afraid—"

"Do not be afraid of me, guardy; there's not the least reason. I've been too long on this track to give it up for any small game," said the Don, for some reason smothering his anger. "All I wish is for you to contradict any such assertion flatly. And, furthermore, I shall flirt with whoever I please."

"Surely, surely," said the general; "no one can debar you from that privilege; but I am glad, from the bottom of my heart, that it is nothing more than a pastime. I was fond of such things in my youth. I don't want the blood of that American on my hands for nothing," he muttered, savagely, as the Don broke away and hurried up the stairs, impatient to have the interview with Senor Velasquez over, that he might join Dora down in the ball-room.

CHAPTER XVII.

A PRIVATE ARRANGEMENT.

Don Carlos entered the private parlor with less alacrity than was his wont when about to meet Senor Velasquez. He paused for a moment, struck with the altered bearing of the man. "What an admirable Jesuit!" he thought.

Senor Velasquez was leaning over a huge folio that lay open before him, his whole attitude and demeanor that of a humble, sacrificing clergyman.

"The demure hypocrite!" was Don Carlos' next thought; "if he deceives others, he'll deceive me for a consideration." He walked more firmly; the senor straightened himself. Don Carlos exclaimed as usual, "Well!"

"Good news! the very best. I have found her," exclaimed the man.

"The senorita, you mean?" said the don, with a little frown.

"Your pardon; I mean Senorita de Monserate. She is on a farm not two miles from this place."

"Well?" echoed the don.

"I humbly await orders," was the response.

"You say you have seen her? How did she appear?"

"Very happy; entirely contented," replied the cunning senor, delighted, as he marked the effect of his words on the darkening brow of Don Carlos.

"Where is she?" he asked, shortly.

"At the house of her—I beg pardon—at the home of a Farmer Goreham—a man of much wealth, I suspect."

"I thought as much," muttered the don, his hate of Los Americanos gaining the ascendency again.

"I have further learned that the old farmer has gone to Washington to get up sympathy and an expedition for his missing son."

"He has!" Don Carlos set his teeth together. "Then 'tis time something was done."

"That is my view of the matter," said Senor Velasquez; while the don seemed deep in thought.

"You are sure she don't know you?"

"Very sure; she rarely looks at a stranger, however—she is suspicious. Perhaps you would like to hear how I have managed?"

"No, no!" replied the don, impatiently; "none of the *modus operandi* for me. It was to escape that that I hired you. Now we have got to think how to act next, and, I confess, my brain is at fault."

"Perhaps you had better leave it with me; I have thought of a plan, if you will hear it."

"Not now, senor. On second thought, I will leave it with you; and here is a little keepsake that will, perhaps, help you out;" he placed a roll of bills in his hand. "She must, at all events, return to Cuba. I'll punish her, at any rate," he muttered, under his breath.

"Yes, I had supposed that—I have arranged for that; it was my first thought; and, to-morrow, I shall go direct to the city to engage a vessel. It is necessary that I should act with dispatch."

"Just go upon your own credit, then, and spare me the whys and wherefores," said the don, impatient to get below-stairs. "Remember, I leave every thing to your sagacity. So, good-night, and come to me if you need help."

"Cool," muttered the senor, as the don hurried away; "the rumor is, after all, true, I imagine. Good! so much the better for me."

He glided quietly down the stairs; stood a moment searching the gay room below, till he caught sight of a glittering couple who had eyes and ears, too, only for themselves; then, with that strange, sneering smile, he left the hall, and hurried away, intent upon villainy.

The next day, as the captain of the bark Aspinwall (a vessel lying at one of the New York piers) sat in his cabin, writing, a formal-looking man, attired in clerical style, called upon him to engage a passage to Cuba.

"I had not thought of taking any cabin passengers this

trip," the captain said, doubtfully. "We are not exact.y prepared, as we are going only with merchandise."

"That will make no difference," replied the man, drawing
from his pocket a purse heavy with gold. "I find that your
vessel leaves here sooner than the steamer sails, and that she
is a clipper-bark, and a very fast sailer. I am placed in
somewhat peculiar circumstances, having in charge the daughter
of a very dear friend, and who is unfortunately laboring under
a slight attack of insanity. She left her family in Havana,
and with only money enough to pay her passage, came to this
country. Fortunately she met with friends, who saw at once
what her condition was, and attended to her wants, placing
themselves immediately in communication with her parents,
who were almost distracted, both being ill on her account. I
was immediately apprised of the fact, and provided with sufficient money to meet all expenses, for her parents are the
wealthiest people in Havana, and she an only child. Thus you
see how I am placed; and, feeling for the agony of my friends,
I wish to dispatch the business with all possible celerity. I
think we must sail with you; as for ship-stores, I can lay in
enough for her wants and my own. Shall I engage state-
rooms?"

"The case is an urgent one, I confess, and makes a strong
appeal to my humanity; still, the idea of having a lunatic on
board is not pleasant. She'll try to jump overboard, or kill
herself, or somebody else, and then there'll be the deuce to
pay."

"I stand ready to be responsible if any violence is attempted, but you may make yourself perfectly easy on that score.
She is not by any means dangerous; a mild melancholy is the
chief symptom in her case. She labors under the delusion
that all who attempt friendliness are her enemies, and she is
chiefly anxious to impress upon everybody the idea that she
is perfectly sane—a favorite ruse with such persons, you
know."

"Yes, yes; I know," answered the captain, quickly; "but,
of course, you won't expect me to run such risks without a
consideration?"

"Of course not; whatever your charges are, I will pay
them willingly and on the instant. I wish for the lady the

largest state-room you have; for myself, the usual accommodations will be sufficient. I am an old voyager. When do you sail?"

"On Friday of this week," was the reply.

The man's olive cheek paled a little. "Good Friday," he muttered; "it would be the worst of luck to sail on that day. Is it imperative?" he queried, in a little lower tone.

"Absolutely!" was the rejoinder. "Her papers said Thursday, but I have been obliged to put off a day."

"Another ill-omen," muttered the seeming minister.

"We Yankees regard such signs as of little moment," said the captain, bluntly; "they belong to the times when witchcraft abounded, and they hung a pretty girl for making faces. As far as luck goes, the Aspinwall has never made a poor voyage; her reputation is up as a first-class go-ahead vessel, and I'd stake a good deal on her for five years to come, if I were a betting man."

Still that ominous cloud rested on the Cuban's brow. He had been nurtured in superstitions, that took a strong hold upon his imagination, and that could not now be rooted out. But time was passing, and the work must be done; every thing, as he had told Don Carlos, depended now upon dispatch. He finally closed his business with the captain, stating that the young lady would be brought on board probably near evening; that he should prefer to have a clear gangway, that her condition might not be suspected; finally, that being young and beautiful, she might work upon the captain's sympathy; but that positively as they would show (he here pointed to some forged testimonials which he had presented for the captain's inspection), the matter was as he stated it; all of which the captain readily believed, with the more faith, as he felt the hard gold under his hand. So, it was settled that on Friday, the Aspinwall would leave port with three passengers the Cuban, Senorita Minerva, and a maid for the latter

CHAPTER XVIII.

AN ABDUCTION.

MORE than a week had elapsed, and Minerva sat at the window of her large cool room, reading one of Jessie's innocent letters. She was having such capital times. "Oh! Minerva could not begin to imagine how happy she was. She found that her uncle, though very rich, was not at all proud," she said, "and his daughters, though they were educated at the convent (didn't it seem funny, though?) were as good Protestants as she was. And, oh! she had actually seen and shaken hands with the President; had been to the White House with her cousins, and such an array of splendid dresses, fair faces, and noble-looking men, she never saw before. She had visited every place of interest, had been to two or three parties, and oh! she was perfectly wild with pleasure. But the best of the news, and what she was sure would seem to Minerva more glorious than all, was, that the men with whom her father held audience, were to see what they could do in the case of dear Herman. There had been so much fuss, of late, with fillibusters, and all that sort of thing, that they supposed he might be imprisoned by the officials of Havana, or be the victim of private malice; in either case, they would do what they could." Then followed words of love and caution, so that Minerva sat with tear-filled eyes, quite happy, looking out upon the beautiful prospect. Her faith in seeing Herman again had strongly revived—perhaps I should say *strangely* revived, by as simple a thing as a dream. She had heard his voice—the tone was that of gladness. She seemed to be brought to his side as by a miracle; to her he looked for hope, for help, almost for life. Never had her heart beat with such mingled emotions as when she awoke from that vision. She was so happy! she felt almost as if wings had replaced her slower powers of locomotion, and she could hear still the whisper of his voice through the quiet air

The time was 'after dinner, nearing three o'clock of the fternoon. When she had read Jessie's letter, she hurried into he room of Mrs. Goreham, who was partially an invalid.

"Are you well enough to walk, this afternoon?" she asked.

"Not quite," was the reply. "But don't stay for me, your exercise is so limited, that I dare not have you give up your walk. Take Bruno, and I am sure the gardener's wife will go with you."

It was a lovely afternoon, and Minerva longed for the solitude of the great oaks, where she was wont to rove. Truth to tell, it suited her best to be alone, though the company of the good farmer's wife was no intrusion, for her tastes were refined, and her conversation was instructive. She left the room silently to prepare herself, and on the way met the gardener's wife, who to her response: " *Be* you going out?" received no reply, save the quiet, "yes;" for Minerva could not run the risk of spoiling a lovely walk by the common-place society of the fat gardener's wife. So, after throwing on bonnet and mantle, she sauntered through the long, shaded entry, out upon the shadowed grass plat, covered with snowiest laces, and called Bruno. At the sound of her sweet voice, the dog, who was lying near his house, at the farther end of the garden, sprang up with a joyful cry, and ran toward her. She patted him on the head as she stood there, a pretty picture, her dark curls blown about her check by the breeze, and the dog with half-human eyes, fixed upon her beautiful face.

"Bruno, will you go with me for a walk?" she asked, showing the little book that she usually carried upon such excursions.

The dog gave a sharp bark, that might have been interpreted, "yes."

"Well, come along then, but you must not run; here, here, stay close beside me, for I have no other protector but you, to-day."

The faithful creature surely understood, for he fell back on the instant, and moved with her step for step, looking momently up as if he said, "you see I am trying to take the best of care of you." Quietly they walked along the grassy path that led to the broad fields. These they passed, under the shade of the apple-trees that lined either side. The low hum of

insects in the under-brush and along the hedges, the quick, soft twitter of birds in the branches overhead, the ripple of a brook not far off, all these combined to add to the delightful reflections with which Jessie's letter, so sweet, so guileless, had filled her mind.   They passed here an orchard, with its wealth of ripening fruit, there a patch of some choice vegetable, and again, a field of waving corn.   Presently, the paths became more like roads.   A thick and pleasant foliage came soon in sight, and the cool smell of the groves greeted the senses deliciously.   A light stile taken down—Bruno had leaped it previously—and Minerva was in her favorite haunt.   How silvery green the trees were, with the sun sending, between their branches, soft pencil-rays of light !   Far as the eye could reach, there was a roofing of green, for here the beautiful elms had been trained in arching sprays, that met, forming lines of beauty.   Away, on every hand, these cool, dark paths extended, and seats were placed at intervals, for resting places.   Minerva strayed on, smiling to herself, and talking to Bruno for growling, as he went.

"Bruno, you're a bad, naughty boy; did you know it, Bruno ?   And Bruno, I shall report you to your master, when he comes home, your *young* master, I mean ; fie, fie, stop growling, you ought to give a laugh-bark, when I speak of him, did you know it, sir ?   I wonder if you'll remember him, you bad boy ! of course you will, though, a year's absence doesn't matter much to a dog, does it, Bruno ?   What ! growling still ?   What is it at, I wonder ? at the beautiful pieces of blue sky up there ? or the scent of these sweet wild flowers ? for shame ! a great, intelligent dog like you, to see nothing lovely in this charming place ! Is it a snake, Bruno ?   I wonder what can ail the creature ?   He has done so three or four times, lately.   Who's here, Bruno, good dog ! you'll protect me, won't you ?   Yes, yes, fine old Bruno, only I don't half-like that growling," she added, musingly.   "Of course there's nobody here, but I'm nervous, I believe, nevertheless, ah !"

She uttered a short, shrill scream, and sank back, pale, almost helpless.   The report of a gun had sounded near, and alas ! Bruno, the good, noble dog, had rolled at her feet, covered with life-blood.

"Oh, my God, protect me!" cried Minerva; "Oh, Heaven, which way shall I go?"

"Not that way, for your life," cried a deep voice, and in another moment, the man in green spectacles stood before her. "Pardon me, madam," he added, in a tone of deep respect, and pointing to the path he had come; "I think there are villains there. Some one is lurking round, this poor creature is a prey."

"Oh!" Minerva shuddered; "what shall I do? I have enemies, dreadful enemies, which way must I go to escape them?"

"Will you trust yourself to my guidance? your friend at the farm-house, Mrs. Goreham, delivered this key in my keeping, that I might have an opportunity to inspect the place."

Minerva felt comparatively at ease. Surely Mrs. Goreham would never have lightly done a thing like that, unless she had perfect confidence in the man.

"If you will conduct me home, safely," she said, trembling in every limb, as she accepted his arm, glancing with so innocent, supplicating a look in his face, that his heart must have been a stone, to resist its pleading.

"There is a road not far from here," he paused to listen, as if suspicious that some one was near, "that leads into the public highway; once there, you are safe:" all this time he was leading her rapidly.

"I seem to hear horses' feet," she said; "I am full of terror, oh, it was so cruel to kill poor Bruno! how could they have the heart? Why! here is a carriage in the private grounds, what does it mean? I—" a sponge applied to her lips and nostrils, cut short the sentence, the door was opened, the unconscious girl lifted in, Senor Velasquez entered after, the door slammed to, the vehicle was driven rapidly out, a boy posted at the stile, with a key, locked the gate and threw it into the carriage; in return, the senor tossed him a piece of silver.

When Minerva again came to consciousness, she lay on a bed in the captain's state-room, which had been given up and arranged for her. There was the eternal sound of the waters beneath, the plashing against the vessel's side, the swift, uneasy motion. After a moment of bewilderment, she closed her eyes with a smile, murmuring, "Thank God, it was then only a dream, and we have started, and Herman is on board--"

She glanced slowly around the cabin. It certainly was different in size and appointments from the one she had gone to sleep in. Bewildered and surprised, she tried to gather her thoughts, as she murmured, "If only Bandola would come in, then I should know; if my head would only stop aching, and Bandola would come."

The door opened, for a moment her heart beat violently, but sank again when she saw enter, not Bandola, but a stout negress, whose face was most unpleasant.

"It was no dream, then," she murmured; "it was no dream, Oh, God, help me!"

"What's the matter, chile?" asked the woman, standing off, as if not quite decided, whether it was safe to approach nearer.

"They have brought me here against my will," she cried, bursting into tears, and striking her forehead with her clasped hands.

"They always says so," muttered the woman. "Well! so long you's not wiolent, you'll fare well, chile, but ef you begins to git wrathy, the Lord help ye! ye'll have to have straight-jacket right on, no mistake."

"A straight-jacket—me? oh! what *can* you mean?" cried Minerva, white with new and sudden terror.

"Never mind, honey, on'y try to keep right, dat's all. The man as brought you here, told me jest what to do, so you needn't talk none, honey, no use for you to tell ole story, you knows, might's well keep yer grief to yerself."

"God help me! I don't know what you mean," said Minerva, quite despairingly.

"No, no, you never does," said the negress, shortly; "I've seen 'em in irons and jackets and every thing, an they never knows what it's for."

A little light began to glimmer on the poor girl's brain.

"Where are they taking me?" she asked, faintly.

"To Cuby, chile, back to your old father and mother, breaking dere hearts for ye, honey."

"I haven't any father and mother, they both died years ago."

"Oh, no! I 'spects not," said the negress, pleasantly, laughing a little to herself. "If I'd said they's dead, 'spoze you'd a thought 'em living, eh? But, don't make no difference, no-ways, you's going back to Cuby; 'spects you never was in Cuby, neither."

"Oh, yes! that was my home, I was born in Havana," said Minerva.

"Well, that's mighty reasonable, now, considering, thought as maybe you wouldn't recollect, p'raps."

"I recollect too much," murmured the young girl, grievingly. A moment after she said, "Can I not see the captain?"

"Well, I guesses not, captain doesn't like to go in ladies state-rooms; if you wants de steward now, he'll bring you any thing you orders. Say, piece of grill chicken."

"Oh, no, no, no," exclaimed Minerva, in tones of intense disgust. To think of food in her misery, was too much.

"Well, I doesn't insist on nothin'," replied the negress; "'xcept ye must be very quiet and still, 'cause there'll be no danger to ye, if ye be; but, I've known some folks in your state, to be let right down in the water, when de paroxisms come too strong, so try to be still, honey."

"What is your name?" asked Minerva, after she had watched the woman with pitiful eyes for some moments.

"I's called Mrs. Roxy," was the reply. "Well, chile, stop looking at me, yer eyes kinder haunt me; what is it you wants?"

"Oh, Mrs. Roxy," murmured Minerva, plaintively; "won't you leave me for a little while? I should like to be alone for a short time."

"Orders is to watch ye close, chile, see't you don't do no mischief," was the short reply.

"But you needn't be in the least afraid, I'm persecuted by wicked people, who wish to injure me; I assure you, I have all my faculties, I know all about it, and I shall submit, because I must. I am in the power of bad people, and must wait till God delivers me out of their hands."

"All sounds wise and natcral," said the negress, "but I ain't no fool, I tell ye, I's seen people jest your way; ye'd never know 'twasn't jest as they said, if 'twant for 'sperience; you see, chile, I's got 'sperience."

For a moment, Minerva was hopeless, but after she had thought a while, she said:

"Will you let me write something with a pencil, and will you give it to the man who brought me?"

"Oh, yes, anythin' in reason, honey; I ain't 'clined to be onreasonable," was the reply.

Minerva lifted the little gold pencil attached to her chain, and wrote as follows:

"SENOR VELASQUEZ:

"*For it must be you*, although your disguise deceived me thoroughly; you can perhaps contemplate the act you have performed with complacency. I leave you and your conscience with God, who is the Judge and the Father of the orphan. I only beg you, as you hope for mercy, hereafter to let me be alone, whenever I wish. The face of the old servant who attends me is disagreeable, I do not want her in my state-room. Say what you will to them all, I shall put my case in the hands of God, and leave with Him, also, the retribution; but let me not be annoyed with any attendance.

"MINERVA DE MONSERATE."

The negress carried the note. In a few moments she returned, looking somewhat crest fallen. In her hand she carried a folded paper, on which was written:

"Your request shall be complied with, I have given orders."

The young girl smiled bitterly.

"I knew he would not dare to do otherwise," she said to herself.

CHAPTER XIX.

TROUBLE AT THE FARM-HOUSE.

THE rays of the declining sun made faint show in one corner of the farm-house kitchen. The farmer's wife had not long been awake from her nap; the cook was busy frying griddle-cakes; the gardener stood outside, mending a damaged hoe; the gardener's wife, who was fond of the good things of this life, had taken a cruller from the well-heaped pile upon the supper-table, and was devouring it with much zest. The whitest of white linen cloths graced the board. It was spread with taste; and honey and grapes, and golden butter and rich cream abounded.

The kitchen, with its venerable furniture, never looked more charming; content seemed lurking and smiling in every corner, and the old fashioned high-shouldered silver tea-set, glistened with the very broadest benevolence, as it stood ready to do duty.

"Come, ain't supper most ready?" asked the gardener, who had somewhat improved his appearance by a clean shirt and a whiter face, while his hair was scrupulously combed and parted.

"Quite, I guess," replied his wife, seizing the bell that stood near, and ringing it with some vehemence.

Mrs. Goreham came into the room, looking at the little, old fashioned gold watch she always wore of afternoons, and walked quite primly up to the table, to survey its appointments,—her daily custom.

"How pleasant it will be to see the dear faces again," she said, quietly preparing to seat herself. "Why doesn't Miss Minerva come, I wonder; do you think she heard the bell?"

"La, yes, she must," replied the gardener's wife. "Come to think on't, I haven't seen her come home. 'Spose she got asleep in them woods? No harm though, if she did, with Bruno to watch her."

"Oh, of course she came home," said Mrs. Goreham, confidently; "she never stays. She might have come in some other way; just ring again, if you please."

Again the bell tingled—no answer.

"I'll go and see if Bruno's here," said the gardener, while the farmer's wife sat irresolute.

"Might as well say grace, Miss Goreham, p'r'haps by that time she'll come. She laid down, like's not, and fell to sleep," the gardener's wife said, cautiously. "There's Mr. Hambledon at the yeller house, when the folks don't come in time to the table, he begins to say grace, and you ought to see how it brings 'em. He never waits, for what's the use?"

"I'll wait a few moments," said Mrs. Goreham, quietly.

"Well, it beats all," exclaimed the gardener; "Bruno ain't nowhere. I called him with a whistle, as he hears gen'ally from one end o' the farm to the t'other, but I don't see him."

"What can be the meaning of the child's stopping in this manner? The sun is almost down," exclaimed Mrs. Goreham, an indefinable terror taking possession of her heart. "I should have known better than to have let her walk alone. I thought you would certainly go with her," she added, turning to the gardener's wife, who was quietly helping herself to another cruller.

"She never so much as asked me," replied that portly personage. "She has too high ways for us humble folks."

"She did not? and I would not have sent her by herself, for worlds. How imprudent! we must make immediate search."

"Bless my heart!" exclaimed the gardener's wife, watching the hurried efforts of Mrs. Goreham, who was throwing on bonnet and shawl, "ain't she old enough to take care of herself?"

"She is placed in peculiar circumstances," replied Mrs. Goreham, in a quick voice; then signifying to the gardener (who, meantime, had swallowed a cup of tea, poured expeditiously by his wife, managing at the same time to fill his pockets with doughnuts), they went away together, the man not forgetting to provide himself with a stout stick. In silence they walked at a rapid gait, till they reached the entrance of the resort that was Minerva's favorite resting-place. Slowly and with faltering steps, Mrs. Gorcham moved on, an impression of coming trouble, gaining on her mind with every step she took.

"Oh!" she cried, her face pale with horror, as she came to the motionless body of the dog; "there has been foul work here; Bruno, my poor, faithful Bruno, dead; and Minerva—where is she?"

"That dog's winged, and no mistake," said the gardener, stooping over the prostrate animal, while Mrs. Gorcham, speechless with sudden fear and sorrow, stood like one bereft of consciousness. "He ain't dead, though," he said again, lifting himself; "we'll see if we can't bring him round. But what are we going to do about the young lady?"

"We must search, John; search from one end of the place to the other. You must go home and get men and lights—oh! that ever I should have been so careless; I knew what danger threatened her, too. We were both too secure in our fancied safety; now, Heaven only knows where she is. There has been foul work."

As soon as it was possible, a number of men, principally farm-hands from neighboring places, set out to explore the premises. Until late at night they searched with lanterns, but there were no traces of the young girl visible. The dog was comfortably placed in a cart and driven home, still breathing, but apparently wounded too dangerously to recover. The fright, and the sorrow consequent on this mysterious affair, prostrated the farmer's wife, and hastened the farmer's return.

Jessie came from the brilliant society of Washington to the darkened room of the sick wife, and the sorrow of finding the friend she had learned to love, thrown upon the terrible mercies of her persecutors. After some consultation, the old farmer, whose suspicions had been more than awakened in the direction of the great people at the hotel, decided to go, and, as he expressed it, have a little honest talk with them. He was, accordingly, ushered into the great parlor, during the don's morning lounge, and where the general made it a practice of reading the news. Don Carlos was, as usual, stretched in a silken laziness, puffing slowly at his meerschaum. The don had the civility to nod his visitor to a seat, and then,

with a stare of cool impudence, awaited his communication.
"I have come on the behalf of a young lady who is a
countrywoman of yours," said the farmer, sitting entirely at
his ease, and returning the don's cool stare with a glance every
whit as cool.

"Ah!" ejaculated the Cuban, while the general's newspaper
rattled as he turned it; "what does the young lady wish?"
and he puffed again, this time regarding the ceiling abstractedly.

"I can not tell what she wishes," said the farmer, whose
warm feelings were rapidly getting the better of him; "but,
in plain terms, a young lady, by name Minerva de Monserate,
has been abducted from my home, where she was placed for
safe keeping; and, I have no doubt, you know enough of the
affair, to inform me if she is in good hands, at least."

The paper rattled again with an exultant motion, while the
don, very slowly removing the pipe from his mouth, turned
contemptuous eyes upon the farmer, as he said:

"Old man, what do you suppose I know about young ladies who find an asylum at your house?"

"If I knew as much as you do about it, I think I could
lodge you in an American institution, such as you have not yet
visited," said the old farmer, the hot blood surging to his tem-
ples. "It is my firm belief that you are here under an assumed name, and that you have either abducted the young
lady of whom I speak, and who was to have been married to
my son, for whose disappearance I shall call you also to account at the proper time."

"Old fellow, you are insane," said the don, rising, and inso-
lently stretching himself.

"Don't you call me old fellow, you rascally foreigner," cried
the farmer, advancing toward him. "We American citizens
do not allow even Spanish dons to insult us with impunity."

"My good man," said the little general, fiercely, "do you
know who you are talking to?"

"Well, yes, I believe I do," replied the farmer with bitter
emphasis, standing very straight, and looking terribly grand.
"I am talking to men who call themselves *gentlemen*, but
have never learned to treat gray hairs with respect. I'd whip
my dog Bruno, who is but a brute, if he had so little manners."

"Shall I ring for my servant to show you the way out?" queried the Cuban don, languidly.

"Ring for what, you puppy you!" thundered the old man, in tones that drove both the general and the don some paces backward; "ring for your niggers to show me out? If you dared do it, I'd pitch them and you out of the window;" and his great muscles and strong chest quivered for the action, as he threw his arms out. "You'd look well ringing for your servants to show me the way over my own land. The ground these premises stand on (he stamped with his foot) is mine every inch of it; and you and your niggers, all sold, together, wouldn't bring what it's worth to me. You had better take care how you insult a man who is king on his own soil. I came here peaceably, to ask you a civil question, which you haven't attempted — no, nor haven't *dared* to answer, yet."

"Come, we want none of your pretensions," exclaimed the don, sauntering a little as if elegantly indifferent. "We are accustomed to the privacy of our own apartment; and, in Cuba, between *gentlemen*, the sword would have settled any question of this kind before now, if such words had been employed. You put me under the necessity of ringing my bell."

Like a lion with glaring eyes, the old farmer (who had probably never heard a dislespectful word uttered in his presence), stood for one moment, his brow flaming, his lips looked like iron, his chest dilated—then, it seemed almost without moving—he gave one lunge, and sent the don off his slippered feet, nearly the whole length of the room; and, before a word could be said, or a motion made, the farmer was outside the door. None would have suspected, to see him nearing his own home, that he had stirred a muscle, or drawn a deeper breath than usual, since he left it an hour before. He felt as if he had done his duty; and, unconsciously, the blow was for his son, whose fate he now, with more certainty than ever, connected with the Cuban aristocrats. At the great stone step he was met by Jessie, who had been watching for him.

"O father!" she cried, "I am glad you have come home."

"Is mother worse?" asked the farmer, standing still.

"No; but there's a gentleman in the parlor waiting for

you, and he has been talking with me this half-hour. **He** knew Minerva and all her family."

The farmer hastened in, followed by his daughter, whose attention had been powerfully attracted by the handsome face of the stranger.

It was Senor Abrates who introduced himself to the farmer. He had heard of the abduction, he said, and, being interested in the young lady, had come to see what he could learn about it. He had been, in earlier years, a playmate of Senorita de Monserate, and both his sister and himself regretted the unpleasant turn which the affair had taken. Understanding, to some extent at least, how matters stood, he believed that the senorita had been forcibly carried away; and the probability of her fate, if she were in the hands of Don Carlos' deceiving agent, filled him with dismay, for he did not believe the latter was at all scrupulous in the fulfillment of his engagements, nor could he believe him under oath.

This testimony placed matters in the most unfavorable light. Tender-hearted Jessie walked to the window to hide her tears, and the old farmer, resting his cheek on his brown hand, mused silently. At last he said fervently:

"Well, I believe I'm one of the Old Testament Christians, for I'm dreadful apt to take judgment in my own hands where I think the Lord allows it. And I've got the faith of those times, too, as well, for I believe the God of Moses will protect that poor child; ay, and bring my son back to me from a foreign land. It may not seem consistent to say that I shall pray for this, when you may hear, maybe, that I knocked down that Spanish puppy at the hotel up yonder for his insolence; but my blood is quick, and the man deserved it. Think of his calling his *niggers* to order me—*me* out of his room. I'd do it again."

Senor Abrates laughed heartily. "That makes the second time," he said.

"Why, what do you mean?" queried the old farmer.

"Your son did the same service for him, so I have understood, when, through his contrivance, he was ordered to prison."

"Ah!" said the old man, thoughtfully, "is that so? Herman was always a plucky boy, but I never knew him to fight

It must have been a great provocation, as is my case; and certainly it is the first time I have ever laid hands on any man."

It is needless to say, that after the interview with the young Spaniard, who promised to leave nothing undone in this matter that he could do, the old farmer suffered some remorse for the deed of the morning. His conscience, quick and clear, took him to task, in spite of his self-gratulations on his old-fashioned religion—" an eye for an eye, a tooth for a tooth."

CHAPTER XX.

THE END OF SENOR VELASQUEZ.

THE voyage to Cuba in the Aspinwall threatened to prove tedious. A succession of head-winds and baffling storms, that made the captain protest, not always in the most decorous language, that he believed there was a Jonah on board, detained them daily; and, to add to the general uneasiness, the captain had Senor Velasquez on his hands, sick with what threatened to be a dangerous fever. Day after day Minerva remained in her state-room, until the captain, thoroughly alarmed for his patient, and believing, from the incoherent self-accusations he had listened to, that Minerva's story was the true one, run the risk of her sanity, and sent for her. After some conversation, his brow cleared.

" If I had known this sooner," he said, " I should have let the villain die, for he is not fit to live. Here I have been nursing and doctoring him, giving him the time my duties absolutely required, and all for a lying impostor."

" What can I do ?" asked Minerva, anxiously; " I am tired of inaction. Let me aid you in some way."

" You," exclaimed the captain, with some vehemence; " I'd see the wretch rot before you should help him. What ! after he has tried to murder you by inches ?"

" I am required to help my worst enemy in his need," said

Minerva, gently. "That, at least, I have learned in all my troubles : to cherish no malice, and to return good for evil."

"Well, I'll be blest, then, if you ain't a thorough-going Christian," said the sailor, in his rough way; "nothing else could do it—no," he added, *sotto voce;* "and, even then, nothing else but a woman !"

So, when she was able, Minerva took her post by the state room in which Senor Velasquez lay. Frightfully changed he was in the short struggle he had had with the fearful typhoid. When the delirium was on him, he talked much of Minerva, and exposed his plans with diabolical minuteness. One night, Minerva, whose state-room was opposite, heard the name of Herman on the frenzied lips. The moon threw its silvery light in at the stern windows, so that every object was clearly visible, and Minerva, anxious to hear whatever concerned that beloved name, glided softly from her state-room and crept to to the other side of the cabin. The negress, who was employed as nurse, sat on the floor just beyond the door, asleep, her bowed head resting on her folded arms. Senor Velasquez was talking very softly now, so that Minerva crept closer and closer to listen. Terrified at his face, she turned her eyes from the ghastly picture. The steward had shaven his head, and his eyes weirdly wild, large and ebon, rolled from side to side in their loose sockets.

"Yes, yes, Don Carlos," muttered the sick man, "I'll keep the secret of La Vintresse. Are you sure you have him safe there ? Los Americanos are very cunning—very strong ! Ah ! old Jose is with him, the treacherous old dog ! He knows how to torture—let the prisoner look to it—La Vintresse. I was there myself once—heaven preserve me from the recollection ! The walls were half down—rotten posts stood tottering, sunk at their base in pools of mud and water. There was not a green spot—the man will die of desolation. He will choke himself with his own hands; he will beat his brains out against the horrid walls ; yes, yes, he will go mad!"

Minerva listened shudderingly. Presently he broke out in a wild cry—"Bring the priest !" It was a strange fancy, but, nevertheless, it occurred to Minerva to repeat the word "confess."

"Ah !" cried the senor, eagerly, "are you here, holy father?"

"I am." said Minerva, in a low voice.

" No, no—but stop—I see the crown of your head—yes, yes, the shaven head, and the rosary, and the robe;" and here began a confession, now and then coherent—at times too shocking for human hearing, but still the shrinking girl listened in the strange silence that was not silence, for the waves, as they washed up, answered the sick man's moan. At last he came to his later life. "Father," he said, "listen. I wanted the girl, and I was promised a fabulous sum if I secured her to the old general, her uncle. But I was cunning," he added, in a tone of triumph; "I made them pledge the money to me, and, after all my planning and theirs, I meant to marry her myself, and secure the fortune. Half should have gone to the church, holy father, so I should be absolved. I put her on the vessel, I carried her to Cuba, and there the fiends got me. See!" he cried, for the confession had gone from his mind, and his raving grew so fearful that Minerva was obliged to waken both the steward and the captain. Their tardy steps were, however, too late; the state-room was empty, and the black nurse sat crouched up in a heap, her eyes glittering with terror while she cried, "O captain! the devil! the devil!" The man at the wheel averred that something, either man or ghost, came up the cabin-stairs and flung itself over the ship's side. In an instant every measure was taken, every effort made to recover the ill-fated Cuban—tho tool of worse men than himself—but all in vain; the miserable man had gone to the bottom in the midst of his iniquity, with all his sins on his head.

CHAPTER XXI.

LA VINTRESSE AND THE RESCUE.

MINERVA had scarcely recovered from this shock, when the pleasant shores of her birthplace came in view. The scene, however, brightened her drooping eyes, and gave a little color to her pale cheek as she saw the tall Castle Moro; the flags and the signals; the houses so near the water; the innumerable masts of a heavy commerce. Her plans had been well matured. Secure in her very loneliness, she did not fear for their ultimate success. The captain was ready to stand by her, and, indeed, he would not allow her to leave the ship without close attendance. How strange, and yet familiar seemed the surroundings, as she drew near the place of her former residence. But for the bitter reminiscences connected with past scenes, she could have kissed the smooth trunks of the gorgeous palms. The city was unusually silent; it was the fever-season, and, in addition, they heard that the cholera had broken out with dreadful violence. The house, as they drove up the grand old avenue, had a deserted look. There were but few servants left, and the main building was closed. Minerva went round the wide veranda till she came to the kitchen inclosure. A woman, on her hands and knees, was fanning with her breath a few white coals, while beside her laid a bunch of herbs, and a pan of water. In another moment the flame darted up. The servant turned impatiently at the sound of a footstep echoing through the hollow dreariness of the great cook-room.

It was Bandola.

The girl gave a shriek of mingled joy and terror, sprang to her feet, looked on all sides with vague fear, ran toward Minerva, and fell, weeping, on her shoulder.

"Oh! it is you, then! I never, never expected to see you again. It is too much joy—I shall die of joy."

"No, you won't, Bandola; you must live to help me in my plans. Do you want to go back to America?"

"Oh! God knows!" cried the girl. "Do you think I have never given your letter to the consul? It has almost killed me. Don Carlos came on board when the vessel was in port, and what he said I know not; but the captain told me to go with him, and here I have been kept as a prisoner all these months. I know they have been months, though they have seemed like years. I should never have been here, perhaps, only the servants have been sent to the hospital to tend the sick, and the old housekeeper was taken with the cramps, and let me out to give her medicine. But, oh! if *you* should be ill!"

"Don't fear for me," said Minerva; "God will take care of me. Who is in the house besides you?"

"Nobody but the housekeeper—and there! do you hear wheels? It is that horrible Jose. I have seen his face go past my window every day, till I am so tired of it."

"Where does he come from every day, Bandola?" asked Minerva.

"That I don't know. I've asked the housekeeper many times, but I suppose she never knew either, for she never told me. He brings something in a basket, and carries something away; what it is, I know not. Oh! I can't get tired looking at you," she added, in an ecstasy. "Are you sure I am awake? I have frightful dreams, sometimes; but if this is a dream, I want to sleep always."

"You are wide awake, Bandola; so am I. You shall not remain here, but go back to America with me, if all things come right," said Minerva.

Tears of gratitude stole down the dark cheeks of the grateful girl, as she uttered the low, fervent cry, "God be thanked!"

"I must see this Jose; where is he?" asked Minerva.

"Around at the stables, I suppose," was the reply.

"Lead the way to the housekeeper, Bandola."

The girl held up her head, and marched like a soldier.

Minerva stood before the housekeeper, who gave a shrill cry, and seemed inclined to faint.

"Do not be frightened, my good Monte," said Minerva,

soothingly; "you see I have dropped from the clouds. I wish you to give me the keys of the main body of the house."

"Against the orders of Don Carlos," murmured the house-keeper.

"I am mistress, now," said Minerva, with dignity.

The woman unloosed the keys with trembling eagerness, and placed them in Minerva's hand. Bidding Bandola follow her, she entered at once into the long-closed-up passages, and unlocked the business room, where every thing remained just as the general's steward had left it, with a view, probably, to trimming it up before the family returned. Here she sent for the old negro, Jose. He came in very soon, a tall, bony, cruel-faced man, whose complexion, black though it was, seemed to change to a yellow pallor, when he saw what seemed to be an apparition, for he could scarcely persuade himself of the reality of her presence.

"Jose," she said, sternly, "have you come this morning from La Vintresse?"

The man was dumb for a moment. At last he managed to answer that he had.

"What horses are here?" she asked.

"Rose and Charlie," he replied.

"Put them into the carriage immediately," she exclaimed.

"Into the carriage, senorita?"

"Into the carriage, I said; then come back. Be quick!" she added, in a sharp, authoritative voice.

He was gone, absolutely lost in wonder, and did nothing but roll up the whites of his eyes as he muttered to himself: "Wha' in Harry she gwine to do nex'?"

"Carriage in, senora," he said, humbly.

"Very well, I'm going up to La Vintresse; you may drive me."

If the negro's mien was astonishment and wonder before, it was now simply horror.

"You," was all he said, slinking back shufflingly.

"Yes, I, certainly; I am going to La Vintresse. You, comprehend, perfectly, you are to drive."

"You,—to La Vintresse?" he muttered again, his lips scarcely moving.

"I am out of all patience with you; are you so stupid? Either you may carry me there, peacefully, or I shall appea. to the consul to let the police go with me. I am your mistress, now, and Senor Herman is to be brought from La Viutresse, by my orders."

"But he is sick," muttered the negro, with ashen lips.

"Then see that pillows and a bed are placed in the carriage, go, Bandola, and bring them from wherever you may find them. Be quick, girl," she added, her heart sinking, as she thought little she might know *how* sick he was. Still the negro stood irresolute, staring at her.

"Have you taken leave of your senses, Jose?" she cried, threateningly, stamping her foot in feigned passion. The man muttered an incoherent word or two, and went slowly out. A bed was soon improvised, and bearing a few necessary articles, Minerva entered the carriage with Bandola.

"Stop a moment," she cried, as the man was mounting to his seat; "you will want another man to help, in case he will need to be lifted."

"I lift him," answered the man, surlily, and sprang on the box.

"Are you not afraid?" murmured Bandola.

"Afraid, oh, no, good Bandola, I have not once thought of fear," said Minerva, as the carriage rolled swiftly along. "Jose dares not disobey me, it is *he* who fears, I think; he is a hard, cruel man, but I believe now he fears me. He knows I have power to expose him to the authorities, and he will be the abject slave, till I have done with him. But, O Bandola! what we are going to see, I know not; there I fear every thing."

"It is not possible you believe Mr. Herman is there!" exclaimed the girl, shrinkingly.

"Yes, I believe they have buried him alive, but we sha.' know soon, we must be nearing the outskirts of Havana."

"And shall you take him back with you?"

"If it is possible, immediately to the ship," was the reply. "The captain was to have every thing in readiness, and perhaps a doctor on board. We shall not sail for a week, and he will be perfectly quiet there. We are coming to a dreary place," she added, looking out over a prospect where natui

had been subjected to various tortures by fire and by flood!"
"Oh! what a miserable quiet there is here! so unearthly."

In ·truth, the very air seemed as stagnant as the ground.
The gullies in the road were deep with green water, the
stunted palms seemed each to be laboring under some deform-
ity, the fields were arid, and presently the wretched ruins of
La Vintresse came in view, a sickening mass of black and tottering walls.

"Very dirty here, senora," said Jose, as the carriage stopped
at a large out-building; "but if the senora will wait, Jose
get planks and lay them."

In a few moments there was comparatively a dry path.
Minerva, with difficulty controlled her feelings, as she stepped
into the narrow hall of the building, that had for so long been
Herman's jail.

"The senora I hope will not punish Jose," said the negro,
humbly; "he did but what his master ordered."

"You shall not be punished, Jose, only lead me to him."

Up the narrow, dirty stairs went the old negro, applied the
key reluctantly to the lock, the door opened with a harsh
creak. Bandola had placed one arm about Minerva, for what
with vague terror and excitement, she could scarcely stand.
The room was large, bare, with miserably defaced walls, and
high-barred windows. Neither table nor chair, nothing but a
a low pallet spread in one corner, and a camp stool near one
window, as if the prisoner had lifted himself to see the dreary
sight without.

Minerva gave a low, shivering cry. What was that extended on the pallet, ragged, scarcely human? "Oh! can
that be?" she wailed pitifully.

Jose shrank away from her real sorrow. Slowly she went
up to the prostrate figure, half-hoping it might not be him.
The man seemed asleep, though his hollow eyes were not
much more than half-closed. His skin clung tightly to the
bones of his face, and was so painfully bright, that it suggested
the thought of varnish. The beard had grown frightfully
profuse, and fell on his throat and chest, in matted, tangled
masses. Language cannot convey an idea of his extreme ema-
ciation.

"O Bandola!" sobbed Minerva, the tears raining down;

"can he be alive? can he live? oh! cruel, cruel fiends! How could my uncle and Don Carlos bring an innocent man to this? What shall I do? I fear to touch him, he looks so frail; O Herman! Herman! if you could only speak to me?"

"He sleeps good part of his time," said Jose. Minerva dared not trust herself to reply; she knew the man before her must have been as black in heart as in complexion, to see a fellow-being suffer as he must have suffered; there was inherent cruelty in a nature like that. Kneeling down on the wretched floor, she softly kissed his forehead. The motion, slight as it was, roused him. He opened his eyes, glassy and restless; they fell upon the loving glance of Minerva. A singular change came over his face, the whole countenance lighted as if a thin red flame had suddenly run from vein to vein, under that fearful whiteness. He sprang upright in the bed, cried out in a hollow voice: "At last! at last! O God!" and sank back lifeless.

"I have killed him," cried Minerva, as the negro went toward him.

"He's been so two or three times, senora," said the man. "If you will go down stairs, I will get him ready to go in the carriage. I doesn't think he's dead."

Sobbing like a child, giving way to utter abandonment of grief, Minerva went down the stairs, and walked to and fro in the narrow entry, Bandola trying in vain to console her.

"We must go in the carriage," said the faithful girl; "to hold him if he needs. Only think, he will be taken from this dreadful place, it ought to make you happy."

"Oh! but Bandola, I fear I have killed him," cried Minerva, piteously; "it might have all been managed so differently, and now he is dead, dead," she wailed piteously. She was prevailed upon, however, to enter the carriage, where she adjusted the pillows, and sat dreading to see the lifeless form, that a child might almost carry.

Presently it came. Jose had replaced the miserable rags he wore, with the suit that had been taken from him, prison-fashion, when he was carried thither. Still seemingly dead, he lay white and nerveless upon the soft bed prepared for him. He was yet living. The fresh air, the motion of the carriage revived him. Slowly the luxury of his surroundings dawned upon him. He smiled feebly like a child; he had no longer the strength to speak.

Minerva had given directions to be driven immediately to the pier. The captain stood in readiness, the usual formalities were hurried through, and in a short time the poor invalid lay on a bed of down, surrounded by careful friends and the best of nurses. A skillful doctor pronounced his case one of slow starvation and complete inanition, giving it as his opinion that a year's time would scarcely complete the process of restoration, so entirely had all his faculties succumbed. "And I think if you had delayed till to-morrow," he added, "he would not have been alive, the light was so far spent."

Minerva listened in silent gratitude; she had no words, but thankful tears.

CHAPTER XXII.

ALL'S WELL THAT ENDS WELL.

JESSIE sat in the pleasant parlor of the old farm-house, playing a few pleasant chords. Her mother, pale and feeble, listened from her wheeled-chair near the window. There were flitting thoughts in Jessie's mind that found expression now and then in a sweet smile, or else in a profound bending of the pretty head, while the eyes looked thoughtfully far away.

Presently in came the farmer, but a changed man was he. His cheek was flushed—his face serious yet beaming, while in his great brown eyes could be seen the shadow of tears.

"Jessie," he said softly—"Jessie, come here."

The girl arose, paused a moment, seeing that her mother had fallen asleep, then hurried out to meet her father.

He led her rapidly around the path that led to the grape-arbor.

"Jessie," he said, and the girl caught his hand, for the manly voice was smothered—"Jessie—O God—be thanked! your brother is coming home to us."

"What father—what father?" half-shrieked the girl—"Herman—coming?"

"He will be here to-morrow—think—think Jessie—Minerva, the noble girl!" His voice choked again—his breast heaved—he could say nothing more, but sat down quite overcome, his face hidden in his hands.

"O father! father!" and Jessie hid her face on his shoulders, sobbing. It was a solemn joy—broken only by the sweet words "my brother," and "my son."

"Are you going after him, father?" asked Jessie, lifting her tear-stained face to his.

"No, darling—they will be to-morrow in a close carriage. Herman is, I believe"—his voice trembled again, "quite an in-

valid. We must be prepared to see a great change in him.
Minerva says he has suffered terribly—my poor boy! Those
proud Spaniards shall pay for it."

"They have gone home, father."

"Yes, but we can reach them. Now, how shall we tell
your mother?"

"Father, *I'll* tell her," said Jessie.

"Very well, my darling—break it to her as gently as you
can," and with a grateful heart he kissed the fair white forehead.

One can imagine the emotions of the little party gathered
to welcome the wanderer home on that eventful morning. It
proved a clear and beautiful day, and God was not forgotten
for his glorious sunshine, for all his tender mercies. The pale
lips of the invalid-mother moved often as if in prayer. At
nine o'clock, Senor Abrates came over from the hotel, as seldom a day had passed of late that he did not.

Oh! that sound of carriage-wheels! Jessie cannot endure
the silence—she starts forward screaming that Herman is coming. But when she sees that pale being, lifted in the stalwart
arms of his father—that white figure not at all like the brave,
handsome brother who went away—she starts back, trembling
and in tears. A joyful kiss was on the cheek—soft arms
around her neck—it was the embrace of Minerva. For many
minutes the silence was something solemn and heart-breakin'
but Herman laid his poor head upon his mother's breast, and
felt stealing over him the old content of his boyhood. When
words came, the confusion was appalling. Jessie hovered
round the couch, kissing and caressing, while her father
walked the room with glad and rapid heart-pulsings, praying
audibly in thankfulness for this unlooked-for blessing. Minerva knelt down by old Bruno, quite overcome at sight of
him, for she had long thought him dead, and the faithful creature gave a low whine of delight.

The proud but crest-fallen Don Carlos had returned to
Cuba, but before he went, to the extreme indignation of his
guardian, he had made the pretty butterfly, Dora, his wife.
The poor general never held up his head afterward—poor, for
he was now impoverished since he learned through the Senor
Abrates that Minerva had been put in possession of knowledge

sufficient to secure her fortune to her, and that the oath of allegiance taken by Senor Velasquez was not proof against the wild vaporings of a disordered brain. Neither did his uncle dare take any steps to recover the lost heiress, who, in time, made them sufficiently aware that she "knew her rights, and knowing, would maintain." Herman persuaded his father to take no steps towards restitution, feeling fully repaid for h's sufferings in the constancy of his charming betrothed. But those days of sorrow had left and would leave for years, perhaps during life, the traces of their terrible endurance. As for Senor Abrates, relieved of the responsibility of his sister's care, he had, through the influence at Farmer Goreham's, become a changed man, and saw life through a far different medium than that of his recent past. Imperceptibly, sweet Jessie Goreham was taking the place of his old love, and surely a purer, lovelier creature could not be found. He contemplated putting together the remnant of his fortune and buying out some good business in which Herman might be his helper.

In the great mansion of Don Carlos, Dora queens it. The Don is quite fond of her, and though he is growing a desperate lover of pleasure, he allows himself to be influenced somewhat by his bright, wilful little wife. But the truest happiness reigns in the household of the farmer where the pale son and his beautiful bride, make the home an Eden. Bandola has never left her mistress, and probably never will.

A miserable old man rises at eleven in his little old house leading from the Paseo in Havana. He is to be seen generally at dusk—peevish, thin and repulsive-looking—arm in arm with a withered little old woman of some sixty years, walking slowly through some retired street. The house and a pension for both is the kind bounty of Minerva, but the old general is both ungrateful and unthankful, and to this day berates his niece bitterly, because she did not marry the man she detested that he might be enriched. Who would recognize in those two shriveled grumblers, the haughty general, famous at Saratoga, and the little senorita, whose rich apparel was the envy of feminine eyes?

In time Minerva learned what she had never known before. Her father when only nineteen, had loved a Cuban lady, —a Dona Marie St. Lunan. From all accounts, she was very good and lovely, and the young man had adored her. News came, however, while he was sojourning in England for a time, that she was false to him, and following rapidly, the fact came out that she was married. In despair the young man first attempted his life, then thought better of it, and out of revenge married the first woman who would have him—the beautiful English girl, the mother of Minerva. When he arrived at home, he learned the truth of the matter—she had been sold, forced into marriage with a rich old Don. She would never see him till, her life fading away, she sent for him when she was dying. Her only child, the babe of a few months slept by her side.

It was an anguished meeting.

"We have been unhappily parted," she said, "but I have a son and you a daughter! Promise me that if it is in your power, they two shall be united. Thus, through our children we may once more know a true and worthy love."

"I promise," he said.

Thus it came to pass that both children were reared under the roof of General Limenes de Monserate. The old Don was induced before he died (being also a friend of the general), to give the guardianship of his son into his hands, and the will of Minerva's father provided that if the two children, coming of age, married, half the property was to go to General Limenes as a reward for his endeavors, but that if she married any other man, he (the general) should forfeit all interest in the will. There need be no further explanation, of course the reader sees the result.

General Limenes de Monserate is living yet, and so are all the rest of my characters. Perhaps there are those who knew some of them in Saratoga.

THE END.